MORE BOOKS BY PARKER GREY

Boss Me Dirty
An Office Romance

School Me Dirty
A College Romance

Ride Me Dirty
A Cowboy Romance

Rule Me Dirty
A Royal Romance

Double Dirty Mountain Men
An MFM Ménage Romance

Double Dirty Royals
An MFM Ménage Romance

Don't miss Book 1 and 2 of
Parker's *Filthy Fairy Tales*!

Finding His Princess

I don't even know her name, but I swear I'll find her and claim her as mine.

Ten seconds.

That's how long it took for me to decide that this early-morning diner waitress was going to be the next lucky girl to hop onto my princely d*ck. Yeah, I was hungover as f*ck and still wearing last night's tuxedo, but that's never exactly been a problem.

Most of the time I don't even have to *ask*. His Royal Hardness has a reputation that precedes the rest of me, though not by much -- and girls from all over the kingdom and just *dying* for a ride.

Not her.

This girl runs away, and I'm left standing there like an *sshole. Now all I've got is the memory of her perfect body, luscious lips, and devious smile -- but not her name.

To make matters worse, my father is insisting that I settle down and stop embarrassing him, so he issues an ultimatum: find a wife, or *else*.

I know exactly who I want.

But first I have to find her.

Finding His Princess is a *very* steamy, cheesy, and over-the-top Cinderella story that'll melt your kindle *and* your heart!

Don't miss Book 1 and 2 of
Parker's *Filthy Fairy Tales*!

Waking His Princess

"I've never had an orgasm, okay?"

It's the last thing I thought I'd hear from my best friend's
little sister. Princess Aurora is sweet, innocent, untouched,
and *totally* pure - I never thought I'd hear her say the
word *orgasm* at all.

Now that I have, I can't think about anything else. I've had
dozens of women, but every time I close my eyes I imagine
what Aurora would look like underneath me, biting her lip
and gasping for breath.

What she'd look like naked, face flushed with pleasure.

What she'd look like as she screamed my name, nails dragging
down my back.

Her older brother is my best friend. If he found me sneaking
around with his little sister, he'd kill me - maybe literally. We
can't get caught... but she's a drug, an *addiction*, and I can't stay
away.

There's a story that Aurora was cursed by a witch when she
was a baby - that she'd prick her finger and fall asleep, but I
can tell you that's not gonna happen.

Instead, *my* prick is gonna wake her up.

**Waking His Princess is a super-steamy fairy tale with an
alpha prince, a virgin princess, and plenty of instalove,
where everyone lives happily ever after!**

Protecting Their Princess

A Snow White Romance

by

Parker Grey

Cover: Coverlüv
Editor: Sennah Tate
ISBN: 1981529829
ISBN-13: 978-1981529827

CHAPTER ONE

Bianca

Popcorn: check.

Pint of chocolate ice cream: check.

Glass of red wine: check.

Pajamas, slippers, bra off, hair pulled up in a messy bun: check.

It's *finally* time for the season finale of *Gentleman's Choice*, my own personal favorite guilty pleasure television program, in which an eligible bachelor has six weeks to choose his future wife from twenty eager women.

Tonight, Rowan is deciding between Jade and Serena, and the previews have shot after shot of him staring angstily into the sunset, like deciding between

1

two beautiful women is the hardest thing he's ever done. Whatever, everyone knows he's going to pick Jade. It's *obvious*.

I settle back onto the couch in my private quarters, my own little corner of the palace, ready to finally have this night to myself. For the past few weeks it's been nothing but wall-to-wall Voravian independence celebrations, because four hundred and seventy-three years ago this month we broke away from the Holy Roman Empire.

And as much as I love Voravia, and I love being its princess, going to event after event, waving at the people, standing up straight and smiling pretty? It's all *exhausting*. Thank God I can finally chill out, take my bra off, and watch some reality TV.

The cheesy title sequence starts: rose petals fluttering down over the words *Gentleman's Choice*. A shot of a mansion in the hills, attractive people frolicking on the beach. The silhouette of two people kissing in front of a sunset.

"Rowan has narrowed his options down to just *two* women," the voiceover says. "But *which one* will he choose? After all... a gentleman can only have one choice."

I toss a piece of popcorn into the air and catch it in my mouth.

"Will he choose Jade, the fun-loving firecracker?" the voiceover goes on. "She swept him away on their skydiving date, but the two lovebirds hit a rocky patch when she confessed..."

Static flickers through the picture, briefly turning the faces on screen black-and-white, their features distorted, the sound gone.

"Come *on*," I say.

It rights itself, and I toss another piece of popcorn into the air. Living in a stone palace built sometime around the year 1300 *does* have its downsides, because it's not like it was built with the expectation that someday electricity would exist.

"Or," the voiceover continues, "Will Rowan choose Serena, the upper-class sommelier who wowed him with her knowledge of..."

The picture goes black. No static. No *nothing*.

I wait a second, hoping it'll come back and I won't even have to get up. It happens sometimes, when there's wind in the forest, or the ravens get curious about the wires, that sort of thing.

"Come on!" I say to the TV, *again*.

There's a screech of static and the screen sputters to life, making me jump.

But it's not *Gentleman's Choice*.

It's a blurry video of someone in a suit, wearing a huge rubber mask, sitting behind a newscaster's desk.

I'm still on the couch, frozen with popcorn halfway to my mouth.

What the hell?

"Greetings, Voravia," says a gravelly, screechy voice that sounds like a record scratch. "Please enjoy tonight's entertainment."

The figure on the TV holds one gloved hand out, and the screen changes again. First there's a long clip of a bunny, hopping across a field, the footage old and grainy. It's intercut with a homemade-looking video of a rock climber slowly making his way up a cliff, shot from below.

Bunny, climber, bunny. It's somehow incredibly creepy, but I'm wondering if this is some weird guerilla art thing that's supposed to be making a political point I don't understand.

Out of nowhere, a hawk grabs the bunny, and it *screams*. I gasp, making a face, and the video cuts to the rock climber.

He falls. The camera goes shaky, but there are flashes of his twisted body on the ground.

I turn my face away.

What the hell is going on?

I look back at the screen, but it's only getting worse. It's nothing but horrible accidents, dead bodies, animals eating each other.

Cars smash into each other, buildings go up in flames. Someone's drowning, there's a body with a chalk outline, lions tearing into a gazelle while it's still alive.

I grab the remote and change the channel.

Same thing. I change it again.

Holy shit, this is on *every* channel, the same horrifying progression of gore, again and again. But whatever it is, I'm not watching it.

Just as my thumb's over the power button, I'm stopped cold.

There's one last still shot on the TV, the camera slowly panning back.

It's a girl, lying on a bed, blood soaked through the sheets below. She's got one hand hanging down limply, her eyes and mouth open, wearing a fancy ball gown as blood trickles from her lips.

I gasp, my hand flying to my mouth. My eyes fill with tears, and suddenly I'm on my feet, shaking. I feel like the world is rocking back and forth, like reality's been thrown off balance.

It's *me*. The dead girl on the bed is *me*.

I can't turn it off. I can't even look away, I can only stand there, remote in hand, rooted to the spot as I wonder what the *hell* is going on.

That's my face.

That's my dress. That's my bed.

5

That's my room.

Tears course down my face as I quickly glance down the hall, toward the entrance to my bedroom. I'm suddenly terrified to make any noise, because *what if they're in there?*

What if I'm dead already? What if I'm not really watching TV, this is all some sort of vivid hallucination and—

The door flies open, and I *scream*. I don't even see who it is, but I jump away from the couch, remote in hand, and I brandish it at the men who just came in, backing against the wall.

"Princess Bianca, it's me," says the first man, holding his hands up.

I pant for breath, my heart like a jackhammer, and I slowly lower the remote.

"Hans," I whisper.

He's part of my bodyguard detail, a gruff, middle-aged guy who's been glowering around me for a few years now. I've never been gladder to see him.

"Are you all right?" he asks, striding across the room.

I just nod, hands still shaking, and put the remote on a side table.

As he passes the TV, he turns it off, then takes my shoulders in his hands. Behind him, two more bodyguards rush in, one speaking into a walkie-talkie already.

"Just breathe," Hans says, and I inhale a long, shaky breath. "You're all right."

CHAPTER TWO

Beckett

"Did you see this?" Kieran's voice calls.

"Did I see what?"

I drop two ice cubes into a tumbler, then peruse the private airplane's stock of scotch. After the week we just had, I deserve it.

"The television broadcast about Bianca."

My hand stops mid-reach, and I lean back so I can see my best friend, leaning back in the sumptuous white leather reclining seat, looking at his phone.

He knows something about her that I don't.

"What about her?" I say, trying to force casualness into my voice, grabbing the nearest Scotch.

Kieran doesn't answer right away. I quickly pour two glugs into my glass and cork the bottle again, not bothering to put it back.

He's still looking at something on his phone, face dark, blue eyes aglow with intensity, his mouth a hard line. Instinctively, I know that whatever he's looking at isn't good.

"Tell me," I say, my voice lowering as I walk back into the cabin, ice cubes clinking quietly in my glass.

Stop keeping her to yourself, I think. *Even if it's just some news segment.*

"You should probably just look yourself," he says, and hands me the phone.

It's some news broadcast, the blonde, perky-titted anchor telling the camera that Princess Bianca of Voravia is perfectly safe, but in a secret location after the *events* of last night.

"The fuck happened?" I mutter at the phone.

"Just watch," Kieran says. He turns sideways in his chair, leans his elbows on his knees.

We're both still wearing our suits from the trade summit we attended, but ties are off and sleeves are rolled up as we finally make our way back home to Griskold.

I keep watching the broadcast, stomach sinking as I wonder what could have happened that has Kieran so serious and grim.

Well, more serious and grim than usual. My best friend is a lot of things, but 'a ray of sunshine' isn't one of them.

"Here's the video that the hackers released late last night," Perky Tits says.

There's some shit with a bunny, then some shit with a rock climber. They switch back and forth for a minute, and just as I'm about to ask Kieran what the fuck I'm watching, the bunny gets snagged by a hawk, screaming.

"Poor little guy," I mutter.

Then the rock climber falls. It's probably a couple hundred feet, and *that* one makes my stomach clench, and clench harder when the shaky handheld footage shows his twisted, dead body.

"Kieran what the fuck *is* this?" I ask.

He just looks at me, face grim.

Then the gore starts, all in one-second flashes: car accidents, surgeries, some poor asshole getting his head chopped off by a helicopter blade.

I start sweating, so I look away, take a deep breath.

You're safe, you're fine, you're on Kieran's plane, I remind myself.

Not out in the wilderness, fighting for your life.

"Me too," Kieran says, and I just nod.

Then the flashes stop, and it's one long, slow shot, the camera taking its time to pan out.

A girl on a bed.

No. A dead girl on a bed. Blood everywhere.

No.

It's *Bianca*, dead on the bed.

"What the *fuck*?" I shout, jumping to my feet.

"She's fine," Kieran says quickly. "It's not real."

I throw his phone onto the seat, start stalking up and down the aisle.

"What the fuck kind of sick *fucking* joke is this?" I say, shoving both my hands through my hair. "Who the fuck does this sick shit? They should be fucking hanged, I swear I'll do it myself—"

"Beckett," Kieran says, his voice still low and calm.

I just keep pacing, unable to get the image of a dead Bianca, lying on the bed in a blue gown, out of my head. Even if they also said she's perfectly safe, the image was manipulated somehow.

Kieran glances at me, and I glance back at him. Neither of us says anything for a long moment. I just keep pacing back and forth and he sits in his chair, staring at his hands.

Princess Bianca is a bit of a tender spot in our relationship.

We both met her at our friend Prince Grayson's son's christening a few weeks ago. And right away, we were *both* taken by her: dark hair, bright blue eyes, perfect red lips. Skin so pale it looks like she's never seen the sun.

And right away, we knew she was *different*.

Let me back up: I've fucked a whole lot of women. I've fucked a good number of them right here on this plane, not to mention my own jets. The four of us — me, Kieran, Grayson, and our other friend Declan — are notoriously unable to keep our dicks in our pants or sleep with the same woman more than a few times.

But Kieran and I did a little more than that. One night, after getting *really* wasted, we slept with the same woman.

At the same time.

Together.

I've forgotten her name, but I've never forgotten the way she came again and again, completely overwhelmed as we both took her at once. The way she screamed and moaned and sobbed with pleasure, the way she begged us to never stop fucking her.

We haven't looked back since. Until now, maybe, because Bianca's not some girl in a club who'll flash us her tits and suck one of us off in the bathroom.

Bianca's a sweet, innocent virgin with a laugh like bells. She blushes when she says *hell*.

And I'm not sure I want to share her.

"It's some hacker group," Kieran's voice cuts in, silencing my thoughts. "They're famous for doing stuff like this. Been at it for years, mostly harmless shit, though it's been escalating lately."

I grab my scotch again, take a long drink.

"Escalating?"

He's grabbed his phone back from where I threw it, and he's looking down, flicking the screen with his thumb.

"Last year, they claimed to be behind a bombing and a kidnapping in Morgravia," he says, his voice dead serious. "They had some half-baked political reason, but the explosion killed a bystander, and the Prime Minister's daughter was kidnapped."

Oh *shit*. I remember this, vaguely.

"She got returned a week later, after some negotiations, but she would never talk about what happened to her," Kieran finishes.

I gulp the last of the scotch, set the glass down on the bar again so hard I nearly break it.

"Let's fucking hunt them down," I say, pacing back into the cabin. "Let's go. Let's fucking do it *now*, find those slimy bastards and wring their necks, one by one before they have a chance to—"

"So you know where they are?" Kieran asks, his voice still calm and placid.

I don't answer, just pace. Of course I don't fucking know.

"The intelligence resources of every country in the Central European Alliance have been trying to find out who's behind it for the past year, and they've gotten nowhere," he goes on.

"What?" I say, pacing the other way down the airplane cabin. "So we don't do shit? It's *Bianca*, Kieran."

"Fuck no," he growls, his blue eyes lighting from within. "I'm not saying that."

"Well?"

"I'm saying I have a better idea."

CHAPTER THREE

Kieran

"A hunting cabin?" King Edmund rumbles. "My daughter's being threatened by... by some sort of modern day *internet gang* and your solution is a building that's hundreds of years old?"

His cheeks are starting to turn bright red, his mustache bristling under his impressive nose, dark circles under his eyes. Next to me, Beckett sits up straighter, obviously ready to argue back, but I cut in before he can get started.

"That's why it's perfect," I say, spreading my hands in front of me. "It's completely off the grid. Everything is solar-powered. There's no phone, no internet, and that side of Mount Diavolo doesn't even get cell reception."

The king glowers, but his mustache stops twitching.

"She'll be harder for them to find, and even if they do, they can't rig traffic cameras or hack a car's computer system to smash into a building," I go on. "They'll have to come for her the old-fashioned way, and either they won't, or they'll have to contend with *us*."

"The best they'll be able to do is give Alka-Seltzer to a squirrel," Beckett chimes in.

A few of the serious faces around the table smile, very slightly, and I remember why I brought Beckett. *Someone* needs to be charming, and for my whole life, it's never been me. My best friend, on the other hand, has one of those personalities people gravitate toward.

Queen Madeleine looks at her husband, face serious, head tilted, and he looks back at her. Famously, even though he's technically the monarch, he's long said that she's his best counsel.

"They have a point," she says. "Besides, there are advantages to entrusting her to another kingdom."

The king frowns.

"Such as?"

"No one will be looking for her there," she says, simply. "Whatever problem they have with Bianca is likely a problem with Voravia, not with the girl herself. Exploding a building in Griskold may be considerably less tempting to them."

The king looks back at us, still frowning.

"We've been close allies for several hundred years, Your Highness," I say quickly. "I spoke with Prince Julian himself about the matter, and he agrees that the risk to the Kingdom of Griskold is both minimal and happily taken on to ensure the princess' safety."

Beckett and I aren't royalty. Technically, I'm 247th in line for the Griskoldian throne, and he's 266th, but we're merely noble, not royal.

Merely. It's still a pretty good life, not to mention we served in the elite Royal Griskold Guard with the Prince himself, so we both have a direct line to the palace should we need one.

"Hmmmm," the king murmurs, looking at his wife, stroking his mustache with two fingers.

Queen Madeleine turns to us.

"We'll need to discuss this in private with our advisors," she says, perfectly civil and gracious. "Would you mind giving a few hours to mull over our options and decide how to best alleviate this threat to our daughter's safety?"

"Of course," I say, as Beckett and I both stand, buttoning our suit jackets at the same time. "Please take all the time you need, Your Majesty."

The king and queen both stand, extending their hands across the table, and we shake them firmly.

"Make yourselves at home as well as possible," she

continues. "We'll send for you shortly."

And with that, we're dismissed.

• • •

"Where do you think she is?" Beckett asks.

We're both sitting in some sort of waiting area, on matching chairs, a tasteful coffee table piled with magazines in front of us. It feels more like I'm visiting the dentist than the top-secret bunker of Voravia's government, and it's a little strange.

"Not here," I say.

Beckett sighs, putting his hand behind his head. His feet are already on the coffee table, but even if someone came in right now, they wouldn't mind because it's *Beckett*.

"They wouldn't put her with the rest of the government right now," I say. "I'm sure she's off at a separate secure location, being guarded by—"

"I heard you two were here," a female voice says, and my heart leaps in my chest.

Bianca comes around a corner, smiling at us, and plops down on a third chair. Shadowing her are two big, hulking, serious men, so of course I can't help but size them up.

The first one I could take in a fight, easy, even though he might be an inch or two taller than me. He's got the look of a man who could be surprised easily. The second one might be more of a challenge.

But then again, I'm *damn* good at fighting.

"At your service, Princess," I say with a grin.

She blushes, faintly. It's a *very* good look on her.

"We were just discussing whether you were here," Beckett says, taking his feet off the table.

She sits at a third chair, her movements sensual and graceful in a way I've never seen before: the curve of her neck, the slope of her breasts, the slight movement of her hips.

Bianca's beautiful and innocent and wicked and wide-eyed all at once, and the combination's fucking *intoxicating*. I know she's a virtually untouched virgin — she's the princess of Voravia, of course she is — but something about her gives me the notion that if someone could get her into bed, she'd be fucking incredible.

The raw, rough part of me wants to see her on her back, hands clutching the sheets as she moans my name, wants to see her perfect red lips stretched around my cock as her blue eyes water, looking up at me.

The deepest, roughest part of me wonders what it would be like to fuck her on her hands and knees, grabbing a handful of her hair, Beckett in front of her pumping himself into her—

"What did you decide?" she teases gently, her eyes dancing as she looks from one of us to the other, shaking me out of my stupid daydream.

Stop it, I tell myself sternly. *You can't share Bianca.*

She's not the kind of girl you could share, the kind of girl who would let you.

"Does it matter what we decided?" Beckett asks, grinning.

She smirks, her eyes flicking to me.

"Sounds like you decided I wasn't," she says.

"That's what Kieran thought," Beckett volunteers.

"I just thought it was unlikely," I say, tearing my eyes away from her perfect form.

Even though she's just wearing gray slacks and a sweater, it doesn't stop me from imagining every perfect curve of her body underneath, and it's been a few weeks since I saw her last. I'm hard as *fuck* and trying desperately to hide it.

"Well, surprise," she says, eyes dancing. "Does one of you win a bet or anything?"

As she says it, her tongue flicks along the underside of her top lip, and I'm frozen for a split second.

"Too bad we hadn't gotten that far," Beckett says, still grinning. "What should we bet on next time, huh? Loser has to wear a bright pink top hat for a week?"

I scowl. Most of the time I'm more amused than anyone by Beckett, but not *now*. Not when Bianca's life is in danger, not to mention he's currently charming her half to death while I sit here like a black cloud.

"You want to make bets about Princess Bianca's safety?" I ask, leveling a glare at him.

Bianca turns faintly pink, her cheeks flushing slightly.

"I'm not making bets on her *safety*," he says, leaning forward. "I'm just trying to make things—"

A door opens, cutting him off, and a young woman wearing a neat suit steps through it, bowing slightly to the princess, then nodding at both of us.

"The King and Queen will see you again," she says, and my stomach tightens.

CHAPTER FOUR
Bianca

I shift the handle of the suitcase in my hand, shoulder aching as Kieran opens the huge wooden door with an ancient brass key.

Cabin. They said this place was a *cabin*, and while it's definitely not a mansion or a palace, it's considerably fancier and larger than any other *cabin* I've ever seen.

"Lock rusts sometimes," Kieran mutters. "I've gotta just give it a little—"

With a heavy *thunk*, the key finally turns. Moments later, he's pushing the door open.

"There we go," he says, mostly to himself.

To my left, Beckett makes a sweeping gesture with one hand, and I step over the threshold, heavy suitcase still in hand. Beckett follows.

The moment the door shuts behind me, Kieran takes my suitcase, lifting it like it's nothing.

"Sorry about that," he says, his voice still low, all silk and whiskey. "You couldn't look like you were getting special treatment."

I take a deep breath, then let it out, circling my shoulder around as I wonder what the *hell* I put in there.

"Does that mean we're done with these?" I ask, pointing at the blonde wig on my head.

"*God* yes," Beckett says, and pulls a black wig from his own head, tossing it on a sheet-covered couch. "Jesus, it looked like I had some sort of skunk on my head, I don't even know where we *got*—"

"We should have checked the windows first, you know," Kieran says, blue eyes looking skyward as he rubs one hand against his stubble. "Make sure there are no listening devices, none of them are open, that sort of thing."

He looks back down, piercing me with those ice-blue eyes, and an involuntary shudder runs through my core. Kieran is all dark hair, blue eyes, sharp cheekbones, and thick ropy muscles that look like they've been cut from marble. I've only seen him smile a handful of times — unlike Beckett, who never stops smiling — but the way he gives me these long, heated, smoldering looks...

...well, it does something to me. Something deep down inside that I can't exactly explain, but right now, under his gaze, I can already feel my cheeks reddening.

"Relax, no one knows we're even here," Beckett says. "There are no listening devices, there are no drones hovering over the skylights, there's no robot squirrels waiting to blow us all up. It's just the three of us in the middle of the woods."

Kieran glowers even as he slowly takes off his ugly orange wig, and I follow suit with my long blonde one, glad to have the hot, itchy thing off my head.

"I never said there were robotic squirrels," he says, icy eyes still looking around the cabin. "I'm simply saying we've been entrusted with Princess Bianca, and we should be doing our absolute best to keep her safe from the threats to her life, threats that you and I don't even fully understand, if we're being fucking honest."

"Just because I've injected a little levity into the situation doesn't mean I'm not taking it seriously," Beckett says. "Look, we've spent all day traveling on crowded trains and in those horrible wigs, we're exhausted and cranky, how about we all—"

A loud *creeeeak* echoes through the hall, and we freeze. Beckett and Kieran exchange a glance, both suddenly standing up straight and nodding at each other.

Kieran strides to the massive fireplace and grabs

two pokers. He tosses one to Beckett like it's nothing, then moves silently into the hallway the creak came from, melting into the shadows.

"Breathe," Beckett murmurs to me, over his shoulder.

I take in a deep, shuddering breath, but I'm suddenly terrified. I can't stop playing that video over and over in my head: me, in a pool of blood, dead in my own bedroom. Car crashes and train crashes and then a hyper-realistic picture of me, dead, right in front of me.

It's hard to shake the feeling that whoever made that video is already a couple steps ahead of us. After all, they somehow knew I was going to be watching *Gentleman's Choice* that night, and they hacked into the airwaves without anyone knowing.

And they *still* haven't been caught. Voravian intelligence *still* has no idea how they did it, or why they did it, or what they even want — even the *who* did it is still purely theoretical.

"At worst, it's probably a mouse," Beckett goes on, his voice low and genial. "It doesn't matter how tightly you seal up a place. They're bound to get into a house this old, and when we came in we probably freaked them out pretty bad."

I clear my throat, taking another deep breath. Trying not to sound scared.

"Right," I murmur. "That was mice."

"You're not afraid of those, are you?"

I can't help but notice that even though his voice is light and teasing, his thick knuckles are white on the fireplace poker, his shoulders tight.

He's trying to calm me down, I think.

"Mice? Of course not," I say. "I mean, I don't really *like* them, and I'd prefer they not live in my house, but..."

I trail off to the sound of a door shutting, then another opening. Then shutting.

"Kieran's checking all the rooms," Beckett explains. "Standard procedure. Means he didn't find anything."

His knuckles are still white, though, and for a moment we just listen to doors opening and shutting, both of us silent.

Finally, there are loud, echoing footsteps, and Kieran appears again.

"Nothing," he says. "Probably just the wind, or a tree branch. This place is a few hundred years old, we're never gonna know the truth."

Beckett's hand gripping the poker relaxes too.

"All right," he says, looking from Kieran to me and back. "Welcome to our new, temporary home sweet home."

• • •

A few hours later, I'm soaking in the bathtub while the two men make dinner. The provisions are a bit scarce — we'll mostly have to go into the village ourselves to stock up, so we don't arouse suspicion by having things brought to us — but I've been promised something delicious, and since they told me to go relax, I'm just following orders.

Even though this 'cabin' was built a few hundred years ago, it's been in fairly regular use. That means it's got electricity and hot water — solar panels on the roof, since Griskold is very eco-conscious — plus all modern appliances, furnishings, etc.

Well, *relatively* modern. I'm pretty sure that my bathroom is from no later than the 1960s, judging by the hunting-themed wallpaper that shows a panorama of bears, elk, trees, and assorted other wildlife. Everything in here seems a bit dated, though it's all in perfect condition.

And I'm not complaining. Not in a million years. I'm safe and sound, soaking in a cast-iron tub with lavender-scented bubble bath while two strong, strapping, *sexy* men make me dinner.

It's almost enough to make a girl forget the threats to her life.

I sigh at myself, sinking further into the hot, bubbly water.

There are no exploding robot squirrels, I remind myself. *Just Kieran and Beckett, arguing over how to defrost filet mignon the best way.*

I imagine the two of them, both in the large kitchen. Probably talking about something or other, who knows — laughing at some story from the past, maybe figuring out what we're going to do tomorrow.

Maybe arguing over how to make sauce.

The two of them share everything. They grew up together, and then they were in the Royal Griskold Guard together. Since the Griskold guard is world-renowned for being an elite military unit, they were sent off to some of the most dangerous places in the world together, and they fought together.

And now they're back, working together on behalf of the Kingdom of Griskold, and the two soldiers are *notorious* playboys. I once read Beckett brag that he's had over a hundred women, and that's just the ones he can *remember*.

I've also heard that they do *that* together. I don't think they know that I know that rumor — both Beckett and Kieran treat me like I'm a totally sweet, innocent virgin who'd blush at the first mention that sex *exists*.

I may be a virgin, but I know all about those rumors, even if I'm not supposed to. Hell, I *looked up* those rumors out of sheer curiosity, and honestly? I was surprised at the number of women who were willing to confess to sleeping with both of them at once — and those were just the ones who wanted their names in the tabloids.

Go deeper into the internet, and that's where the *real* dirt is. That's where I found anonymous account after anonymous account of threesomes, going into *full* detail.

I should have stopped reading. I shouldn't have ever started, because Kieran and Beckett quickly became friends of mine after we met, and it feels *wrong* to know such dirty stuff about them. Especially now, when they've both volunteered their lives to keep me safe, I feel a little guilty knowing these deeply personal, intimate accounts of their sex lives.

I shift slightly in the warm water, one hand skimming down my body, the rush of water past my nipples making them stiffen slightly.

I read those accounts over and over. I think I memorized parts of the *really* dirty ones, even though I felt guilty for reading them and — honestly — a little jealous. I know I could never do *any* of the things those women described, but... I can think about them, can't I?

I rest one hand on the inside of my thigh, pussy already pulsing with desire even as I wish I weren't, legs already spread apart, mind already drifting back to the anonymous account I read the most... and imagined myself in the most, despite *everything*.

And I can't help but imagine myself in there *again*, in Beckett's bed as he kisses my throat, my legs already wrapped around him, seated. Behind me Kieran is pinching one nipple, his other hand moving down my body to rub my clit, his fingers playing with my pussy lips

In the bath, I hold my breath. I can *hear* them clanking around in the kitchen, and I feel a little bad about what I'm doing yet again.

Gently, underwater, I start rubbing myself, my finger circling my clit slowly, letting the feeling build as I bite my lip, leaning back onto the cool edge of the tub.

I think about the fantasy, about them getting a little rougher. Now Beckett's rubbing my clit as Kieran grinds his thick, rock-hard erection against my back, his fingers moving down the cleft between my buttocks, skimming past my tight back hole.

I gasp out loud. It's just a little, but the sound echoes off the patterned tile of the bathroom, and I clench my teeth together harder, because I *need* to be quiet, but it's *hard*.

Fantasy-Kieran's fingers are inside me now, hard, thick, and calloused, his other hand pinching my nipple hard as I moan into Beckett's mouth. He adds a second and a third, filling me more, and I can feel myself stretch to accommodate him as Beckett's finger work my clit, driving me to higher and higher points of ecstasy.

In the tub, I spread my legs wider, letting my other hand drift down until I'm parting my own lips, rocking my hips forward, sliding my own fingers inside as I bite back another moan. I wish I'd turned the fan on or let the water run or *something*, because it's so hard not to make noise, but every time I do it's magnified tenfold.

Now Kieran's fucking me hard with his fingers, Beckett working me from the front. I'm on my knees, out of control, hips bucking wildly as the two men play my body perfectly. Kieran bites my ear, growls into it.

"You want us both to fuck you?" he asks.

"Yes," I whisper, but I say it out loud, in the tub, and my eyes fly open.

For a moment, I stop, hoping that no one heard, but nothing happened.

I close my eyes again, push my fingers deeper into my pussy, keep rubbing myself furiously.

Kieran pulls my hips backward, his fingers sliding out, and now I'm on all fours, gasping for breath. In the tub I'm biting my lip, forcing myself not to moan, thinking of Beckett's cock bobbing in front of my face, Kieran's cock right at my entrance, the bright heat building and building inside me.

The moment fantasy-Kieran enters me, I come *hard*. I gasp out loud, make a strangled noise kind of like a moan, bite my lip again to stop myself even as I keep going, keep desperately fucking myself. My pussy spasms around my fingers as I think of Kieran in me with Beckett in my mouth, the way I'd sound moaning around his thick cock.

Finally, shaking, I stop. I pull my hands back and stretch my legs out in the tub, face flushed bright red.

I can't believe I did that, I think. *You shouldn't have found that stuff in the first place, and you shouldn't be thinking about it now, either.*

I'm not sure they'd mind, though. I've seen the looks they give me, noticed how they both go out of their way to talk to me at events.

You could tell them, I think. *See what happens.*

Before I can get any further with that thought, there's a knock on the door.

CHAPTER FIVE

Beckett

I stir the pot, putting the lid back on the sauce, check the oven one more time. Kieran is grabbing plates and silverware, dusting some of it off — no one's lived here in a little while — and I think dinner's ready.

It's nothing fancy, just defrosted frozen steaks and boiled veggies, but at least it's food, and I'm *starving*.

"I'm gonna go let Bianca know dinner is in a few," I tell Kieran.

He just nods, gathering forks. Kieran can be a man of few words, sometimes, but there's no one I'd rather have by my side in a pinch.

I head down the hallway, turn the corner, and then I'm in front of the door ringed with light.

Just as I'm about to knock, I hear slight splashing.

A *sigh*. A hitch in Bianca's breath, and I pause.

That sounds like...

No.

I stop, though. I stand outside the bathroom door and listen to the sounds she's making, even though they're echoing and vague, and I hold my breath.

Softly, she gasps. She's breathing hard, almost like she's fighting back moans. I'm getting hard just listening, because if anyone knows what a woman on the brink of orgasm sounds like, it's me.

I shouldn't eavesdrop, but I can't help myself. The thought of Bianca in the bath, pleasuring herself, is overpowering. I wonder if she's using her fingers, or maybe a vibrator. Maybe she's using the showerhead, though it doesn't sound like it.

Is she fucking herself, or just rubbing her clit?

What's she thinking about?

Despite myself, I touch my cock through my pants. The past few days have been jam-packed with planning and travel that I haven't had a single chance to even jerk off, let *alone* find a girl.

Not that I've done very much of that since meeting Bianca. Somehow, it's just... less appealing now.

There's another splash, another gasped moan.

"Yes," she whispers, her voice echoing off the tiles.

God, I'd give anything to know what she's saying *yes* to. I'd give anything to know what she's thinking about, whether she's thinking about me the way I think about her.

I rest my head gently against the door, listening despite myself to the sounds of Bianca getting herself off. I can tell she's trying not to make any noise, gasping and moaning. I wonder if she's biting her lip the way she does sometimes, her perfect red pucker marred by that dot of white.

Then there's a tiny gasp. A moan cut short, a splash, her breathing ragged and harsh, and I *know* she's coming. The thought makes my cock jerk in my pants, and I slide the flat of my hand along myself, one hand on the door, desperately trying to think about *anything* else but the girl on the other side.

It doesn't work. I can't. I can't have Bianca — at least not here, not *now* — but I can't get her out of my mind, either.

I take a deep breath and knock on the door.

There's a surprised splash on the other side, then a long pause.

"Yes?" her muffled voice says.

I open the door just a crack so she can hear me, and as I do there's a yelp even though all I can see are her toes, peeping out of the water.

"Don't panic, I'm not a robot squirrel," I say. "It's nearly dinner time."

"I didn't think you were a squirrel, I thought you

were going to open the door all the way," she says, her voice languorous and teasing.

"I would never, Princess," I tease right back. "Unless you asked, obviously."

Silence. *Shit.*

"Dinner's nearly ready," I say, keeping my tone light. "Dry off and get dressed fast, we're starving."

"I'll be right there," Bianca says, and I close the door again.

You can't have her, I tell myself over and over again.

Not here, at least. Not now.

You'll protect her and that's all.

• • •

Of all the modern conveniences Kieran's family's hunting cabin-slash-mansion has, a dishwasher isn't one of them. After we eat, we tell Bianca to go to bed — the poor girl isn't used to anything like this, and I was afraid she'd fall asleep on her plate — and clean up ourselves.

For the first couple minutes, neither of us says anything. It's not exactly unusual — Kieran's not a big talker — but this silence feels heavy, almost stifling.

Plus, I know exactly what's causing it. The beautiful, delicate, virgin princess who's asleep in her bed right now. The girl that both of us want, but who we can't possibly share.

"I think we should make a deal," I finally say, scrubbing off the pan we used in the oven.

Kieran moves the faucet to his side of the sink rinsing off a handful of soaped-up silverware.

"A deal about what?" he asks, his low voice soft.

As if he doesn't *know*.

"What do you think, asshole?" I mutter. He may be my best friend, but right now I'm exhausted, *frustrated*, and trying to get gunk off a baking pan.

Kieran jams the silverware into the holder on the drying rack with a long, loud sigh.

"What's the deal?" he finally asks.

I rinse the baking pan, glancing quickly toward the hallway where all three bedrooms are. It's quiet and dark.

"Neither of us gets her," I say.

Kieran doesn't answer. Instead he slowly grabs the towel, wiping his hands. A muscle in his jaw twitches slightly, and I ignore it, carefully balancing the baking pan on top of everything else in the dish drying rack.

"You're just saying that because I saw her first," he tells me.

I glance at him. Even though he sounds deadly serious, there's a smile just barely making itself known around his mouth.

"You did not," I say.

"Sure I did," he says, tilting his head slightly, still teasing me. "And you only want to make this deal because you're so afraid I'm going to charm her right off her feet."

That's how I *know* he's kidding. Kieran gets plenty of women, but it's not because he's got *charm*. He's the dark and mysterious type, attracts the kind of girl who think she can unravel him.

Also the kind of girl that likes having her hair pulled while he fucks her. The kind of girl that doesn't mind having her ass smacked, who likes getting a little *rough*.

"So it's a deal, then?" I ask, keeping my voice low as I dry my own hands off, pruny from washing dishes. "While we're here, *no one* makes a move on the princess."

I don't even need to say *because she'd never let us both fuck her*. That part goes without saying.

Kieran holds out one hand.

"Deal," he says. "As much as I don't want it to be."

"Same," I say, taking his hand and shaking it.

CHAPTER SIX

Kieran

I sleep like the dead. I always do when I'm at the hunting cabin. It's so quiet, so isolated, that it feels like not even the nightmares can find me here, and thank God I don't wake up screaming. *That* would really terrify poor Bianca.

Still, I'm first up in the morning. I never did need too much sleep, and my years in the Royal Griskold Guard cured me of any further need I had to sleep in.

It's barely past dawn when I walk into the kitchen, already dressed, and figure I may as well start making breakfast.

I prep the twenty-year-old coffee maker, and soon enough, it's happily percolating and dripping brown liquid into the pot. I boil water for tea as well, just in case Bianca's the tea drinking type. I don't think she is, but I can't exactly remember.

Then I *really* set to work. Growing up, we always had a chef — an entire kitchen staff, actually — but in the guard, it was my turn to cook for all the men occasionally, and it turned out I liked doing it. Even if the hunting cabin doesn't have much in the way of fresh food, the pantry and freezers are well-stocked, so I grab bacon, frozen berries, the ingredients to make waffles.

I go onto autopilot, I've done this so many times, and my mind wanders.

Half of it wanders to Bianca, of course. How right now, she's asleep in her massive four-poster bed.

I wonder if she sleeps naked, her body soft and warm. I think about what it could be like to wake up next to her luscious naked body, slide below the covers.

Crawl in between her legs and lick her awake, lapping up her sweet honey. Bury my tongue in her pussy and feel the way her body responds when I make her come, again and again.

Shit. There goes my cock for the second time already today. I woke up with a rock-hard erection, and since I finally had a moment of privacy, I took care of it.

Thinking about basically the exact same thing: Bianca, naked and warm, moaning my name.

But then there's the *other* place my mind goes: King Edmund's warning when he agreed to our plan, when he told us in no uncertain terms that his daughter was pure, innocent, and untouched — waiting for her wedding night to lose her virginity to her husband and *only* her husband.

The king's not an idiot. He's well aware of the reputation that the two of us share, but he also knew that this was probably the best option to keep his daughter safe.

So he sat us down and lectured us about *tomfoolery* and *hanky panky* and how we had better not get up to any *funny business* with this daughter, because she'd tell him everything.

No *fooling around*. No *necking*.

Yes, he really used all of those words. He may be an excellent monarch, but King Edmund is a little behind when it comes to describing sexual activity.

And of course, during that whole lecture, it was nearly *impossible* to think about anything else. If someone says *don't even think about touching my beautiful, alluring daughter sexually*, what the fuck else is someone going to think about?

I toss some bacon onto a hot griddle, and immediately it splatters fat everywhere, even onto my shirt, and I curse. I didn't bring too many of them with me, and I don't want this one to get even *more* dirty, so

I take it off and toss it over a chair, turning the stove down as I do.

Seconds later, there's a soft padding sound in the hallway, and Bianca comes out, yawning. She's wearing plaid pajama pants and a tank top, slippers on her feet, her dark hair wild around her head.

No bra. I notice *that* fucking instantly, because her top is *just* tight enough for me to see the outlines of her nipples, the lower curve of her breasts. I was already hard, but now my dick swells even more, nudging at the counter in front of me.

Don't look, I tell myself. *Don't think about it.*

Don't think about grabbing a fistful of that hair as she's on her knees, hands behind her, lips around your cock.

Don't think about the way her perfect, full tits would bounce while she rides your cock.

Don't think about the way she'd scream with pleasure if you both...

"Hey," she says, mid-yawn.

"Sleep well?" I ask, turning the bacon over in the pan.

Maybe it's my imagination, but I could swear she looks at my swollen cock for just one moment before walking to the coffee maker and staring at it, her cheeks turning slightly pink.

She just woke up, they were already that color.

Hands off.

*Hands **off**.*

"Are there coffee mugs?" she asks, her voice soft and sleepy.

I flip one more piece of bacon over in the pan, then walk over behind Bianca. She's standing right in front of the cabinet where the mugs are, and I position myself right behind her.

Even though I know I shouldn't be this close. Even though I agreed with both her father *and* Beckett that neither of us would do anything *untoward* to Bianca.

We never asked her what she wants, I think.

I steady myself with one hand on the counter, right by her hip, and reach around her for the cabinet. The very tip of my swollen cock brushes against her through two layers of clothing as I open the cabinet and grab a mug.

I'm an inch from her hair, and her scent only makes me harder. She smells of strawberries and vanilla, warm and enticing.

Before I can do anything worse, I grab a mug with a deer on it, slam the cabinet shut, and back away.

"Here you go," I say, my voice low and gravelly with desire.

"Thanks," she says. "Am I good to just..."

Bianca gestures at the coffee maker, sleepy eyes blinking.

Don't even look at her, I think. *If you interact with her much more she's going to be up against that counter, and you'll be violating every promise you made.*

"Go for it. Coffee's done," I say brusquely, and head back to the stove as Bianca fills her mug quietly.

CHAPTER SEVEN

Bianca

I guess Kieran's not really a morning person, I think.

I can't quite tell what his deal is. The last time I saw him and Beckett, at my cousin's son's christening ceremonies, he seemed different. Not exactly outgoing and talkative, but not so...

...Dark, or growly.

I pour myself coffee, find the sugar next to it, and add a couple spoonfuls. Kieran doesn't even look over at me as I stir the murky liquid, then take a good, long sip as I look out the window over the kitchen sink.

It's late summer, so it's green and leafy out there. Here in the mountains the foliage is mostly darker evergreens with a few handfuls of brighter-green oaks and maples thrown in.

I wonder how long we're going to be here.

A week? Two?

A month?

I take another long drink of coffee as I glance over at Kieran. He's wearing sweatpants with no shirt as he makes breakfast, his muscles rippling in the low sunlight, the hard lines of his chest and abs shifting.

God, he's even got that V that points toward his...

I glance down, forcing my eyes away and back to the window, and turn bright red, taking another long sip of coffee to cover it up.

Kieran's got a massive erection right now, tenting up his sweatpants. That *must* be what brushed against me just now as he leaned over me, getting a coffee mug out of the cabinet. I clear my throat, take a deep breath, drink more coffee and try to ignore the slow, fiery heat moving down through my core.

He could just bend me over the counter right now, I think.

No one would ever have to know. Beckett might not even wake up, and Kieran could push my pants down, slide that enormous cock into me and just take me here and now...

I drain my coffee mug, annoyed at myself for not being able to think of *anything* but sex, at least not with these two around.

But what if Beckett did wake up? Maybe he could join in...

I clear my throat and force myself to stop fantasizing.

"Can I help with anything?"

Kieran glances at me, his gaze sharp and hard.

"There's frozen orange juice," he says. "Think you can handle making that?"

I lean one hip against the counter, glaring at him, a little annoyed that he's so hot *and* being a dick.

"I don't know, do the instructions have big words in them or can even princesses follow them?"

Kieran doesn't answer, just smirks, turning back to the stove.

"There's a pitcher in the cabinet by your feet," he says.

• • •

A bit later, Beckett wanders out of his bedroom, wearing sweatpants and a thin white shirt. Every time he stretches or moves, it pulls against his muscles, and I have to force myself to stay focused on what I'm doing — making the orange juice from frozen concentrate, finding the dishes and silverware and setting the table.

The two of them talk just a bit, but Beckett also goes to the coffee pot first thing, pours himself a full mug, and gulps it down.

"That bacon still good?" he asks Kieran, leaning against the counter.

I move in front of him, grabbing silverware, and as I do, I can feel his eyes on my body. I try not to shiver with the force of his, but I do. Despite myself.

"Of course it's still good," Kieran says.

"You check the expiration date?"

Kieran just turns and glowers at his friend.

"You want to watch me eat a piece of it as proof that I'm not trying to poison you?"

"I didn't say you were *trying* to poison us," Beckett says, grinning. "Just that you might by accident. I can remember an incident back when we were in the service..."

Kieran shuts the waffle maker a little too hard, and waffle batter splashes out as it thuds closed.

"Yeah, you remember *one* incident. Because there was only ever the one, and I cooked for you assholes how many times?"

I'm not really sure what's going on with these two. I've never seen them bicker like this before — until now, as far as I knew, they were two peas in a pod.

Or two cocks in a...

I clear my throat to rid myself of *that* thought, and they both look over at me, expectantly.

"Sorry," I say. "But also, stop fighting."

"We're not *fighting*," Beckett says, still grinning. "I'm just winding Kieran up a bit."

"Well, the princess said quit it," Kieran says, wiping

his hands on a towel, his eyes suddenly smiling. "You heard the girl."

"So she's in charge now?"

I lean against the table and cross my arms in front of me.

"If it gets you two old hens to quit bickering, then yeah, I'm in charge," I say.

Kieran glances back at me, his muscled torso twisting. I force myself to look away.

"Go find the syrup and sit the fuck down," Kieran says, but despite his words he's clearly in a better mood.

"You gonna put a shirt on?" Beckett fires back.

I roll my eyes at them, find some glasses, and put them out on the table.

• • •

Hours later, I'm sitting on an expensive-looking Persian rug in one of the cabin's many rooms, staring at a bookshelf, trying to find something to read.

In the panic of leaving, it somehow didn't occur to me that I'd need some kind of entertainment while I was here — especially because I've got no idea *how* long I'll be here for.

I didn't bring my computer, or my phone, or any electronics, obviously — everyone was terrified that despite the cabin's remoteness, the hackers would *somehow* find me that way. But I also completely forgot to bring anything *else* for fun.

So I've got no books, no crossword puzzles, no *anything*. I don't even have the knitting project that I abandoned long ago, which could at least be something to work on.

And the books here are boring. This shelf, at least, seems to consist entirely of Griskoldian histories, and from the dusty tomes that I've taken down and thumbed through, they're not even the interesting histories.

They're the dry, dull, year-by-year histories of who held what office, what nobleman curried the most favor, what supplies each military division needed and how they got there. If I needed help sleeping, this would do the trick nicely.

I sigh and look at the bottom shelf, hoping that I can do better than *that* at least, but my hopes aren't high.

But then, in the very corner of the very bottom shelf, I spy something else. Something that's got actual colors on the spine and isn't two inches thick.

The Woodsman's Captive.

I raise one eyebrow and grab it from the shelf. I thought it would be some sort of swashbuckling story about, I don't know, a woodsman who takes someone captive, but from the cover alone it's clear that I'm wrong.

Or, kind of wrong. Because the captive is a *sexy* captive.

I've clearly found the cabin's one romance novel, and it's obviously the steamy kind. On the cover, there's a big, burly woodsman, frilly shirt open to reveal bulging pecs and a six-pack, and in his arms is a blonde woman, practically fainting against him, her breasts nearly-but-not-quite out of her dress.

He's got an axe in one hand. There are some trees around.

Actually, he's got dark hair and piercing blue eyes, and... *kind* of looks like Kieran.

There's nothing better to do, I think. It's been a long time since I read a romance novel this old-school, but I get off the floor and settle into an overstuffed leather armchair in the other corner of the room.

CHAPTER EIGHT

Beckett

"What, are you keeping a diary?" Kieran asks.

We're both slumped on the couch in front of the fireplace, though there's no fire going at the moment. It's still too warm out for that.

"I think it's a good idea to keep a record of what happens here," I say. "Just in case, maybe we can look back and see what went wrong, pinpoint our problems..."

Kieran just shrugs. *He's* reading a huge, thick novel, some historical fiction about King Arthur.

Of course Kieran came prepared with a month's worth of light reading. Kieran's always prepared, always cool, calm, and collected. I know he can come across as harsh and cold sometimes, but it's not really true.

"I think there's pen and paper in the study," he says. "Maybe you could get started on your memoirs while you're at it."

"Maybe I will," I say, getting off the couch, even though I'm kidding. I think that writing my own memoirs might actually bore me to death, because I've already *done* all that stuff. Why re-live it?

I make my way through the halls of the hunting cabin and to the study, where, to my surprise, the light is already on.

I crack the door open to find Bianca sitting in one corner, curled into an overstuffed armchair, totally engrossed in a book. She looks up when I enter, then puts the book in her lap and covers it with one hand, trying to be nonchalant about it.

She's obviously embarrassed about what she's reading.

"Found something good?" I ask, forgetting all about the paper and pen, leaning against the doorframe.

"Just a book," she says, her tone a little *too* casual.

"Lucky," I say. "All the books I've managed to find in here are dreadfully boring. I swear there's a whole shelf about the botany of *just this side* of this mountain."

Bianca laughs, still not showing me the book.

"What's that one?" I ask, coming closer.

She curls herself around it a little more, pressing her hand against the cover.

"Nothing," she insists, but now she's smiling.

"Doesn't look like nothing," I say. "Come on, it's not 'The Merry Housewife's Guide to Eliminating Foul Body Odors,' is it?"

"Do I *smell* like I need that guide?"

Fuck no. She smells wonderful, like vanilla and fruit. Fucking *delicious*.

"I can't say I've ever really smelled you up close," I lie. "Is that an invitation?"

Now I'm standing over her, still in the chair. She looks up at me with her bright blue eyes, red lips slightly parted, fingers splayed over the book.

From here I can see the veins pulsing in her neck, the soft rise and fall of her chest, and it does something *wicked* to me. I want to put my mouth on those veins, want to grab her ribcage between my hands, *feel* her breathe.

I want to see my cock between her lips as those perfect blue eyes look up at me, watering as she swallows my—

I take a deep breath, and with every ounce of willpower I've got, *force* my erection down.

Not here. Not *now*. I'll jerk off to that later — that's for damn sure — but not *now*.

"It's a romance novel I found," she finally admits,

taking her hand from the cover. "You know, some trashy old book that was just sitting around."

I raise both eyebrows at the cover, because *that* is definitely softcore porn.

"You get to the good parts yet?" I ask.

Bianca stretches out, sitting sideways on the chair, her feet over one arm.

"I've got no idea what you mean," she teases.

"The hell you don't," I say, grinning. "Did you even read the first half, or did you skip right to 'his member, like steel wrapped in velvet...'?"

"I didn't know you were a connoisseur of romance novels," Bianca says, tilting her head back. "Sounds like you're practically an expert."

"Why wouldn't I read them?" I ask. "When I was a kid, my governess *loved* the things. What better way to learn what women like?"

Bianca blushes, kicking her feet a little.

"Though I admit the euphemisms were a little confusing at first," I say, flipping casually through the book. "I wasn't sure why there were so many delicate flowers and all that, though I figured it out pretty fast."

"That got me too, at least for a while," she says. "And *then* I figured it out, and suddenly..."

She trails off, looking at her toes.

"Suddenly what?" I tease. "You had a passion for gardening?"

"I was even *more* interested in these things," she laughs. "I must have gotten caught with them a dozen times. I even got grounded for it once or twice. My cousin Aurora would sneak them to me, since her parents were a *tiny* bit less strict than mine."

"Speaking of strict parents, I *should* take this away from you and scour the cabin for any more of them," I say. "Your father made us swear up and down to keep you chaste."

Her faces changes instantly.

Now Bianca looks horrified, her face turning splotchy pink, white spots in the very center of her cheeks.

"He didn't," she says.

"He did," I say, suddenly feeling bad for her.

"Jesus," she mutters, looking down and away. "You'd think I was a twelve-year-old nun locked away in a tower. Did he threaten to put a chastity belt on me, too?"

I lick my lips, even though I don't mean to.

"Does that mean you haven't got one?"

"Not *yet*, at least," she says, looking at me again. "Though if my father's making the two of you swear to keep my hymen intact, I imagine it can't be far away."

Every time she opens her mouth, I get harder, I swear to God. Even thinking of her in a chastity belt means thinking of her otherwise naked, nothing but a strip of metal around her hips, plunging down between her legs.

I'm *positive* I could still figure something out, chastity belt or no.

"Well, we both promised," I say, casually flipping the book open again. "So I'm afraid I won't be, let's see, 'invading your love cavern with my masculine pole.'"

Bianca smiles a little, then bites her lip.

"I think that sounds a bit too much like spear fishing for my tastes anyway," she says.

"What about 'spreading your delicate petals with my deft touch, discovering the sweet honeypot within'?"

She blushes, bites her lip harder. The purple prose, courtesy of *The Woodsman's Captive* isn't getting me harder at all — it's just watching *her* reaction to it.

And her annoyed reaction to discovering what her dad said? That doesn't hurt either.

"I never did like the euphemism *honeypot*," she says.

I toss the book onto her lap, cock now at half-mast. I know she can see it, and I don't even care.

"What about *licking you until you come twice, then fucking you until you scream my name*?"

Her eyes are wide, her lips parted. Bianca doesn't answer right away, but I know what a woman looks like when she's turned on as *fuck*, when she's heard

57

something she likes, and this is it.

This is exactly it.

Damn it all to hell. Damn the promises I made to her father, damn the deal I made with Kieran. I fucking *need* Bianca, and if I can, I'm going to have her.

"Is that in here?" she finally whispers.

"How's that memoir going?" Kieran's voice asks from the doorway, and I whirl around to find my best friend leaning there, looking *furious*.

Shit.

CHAPTER NINE

Kieran

He's fucking talking dirty to her. First, he made her laugh, now he's talking dirty to her.

I'm so jealous I can't even see straight. I *knew* it would be like this. I knew she'd want him and not me, because he's funny and charming and I'm... well, I'm *me*.

I've always been like this — serious and straight-laced — and even though it works for me, out in the world, I don't think I've got a chance one-on-one like this.

Beckett freezes for a split second, then his shoulders relax.

"It's going fine," he says, turning casually, leaning against a desk. "Bianca found a trashy old romance novel and we were just laughing about some of the stuff in it."

"It calls a vagina a damp love-cave," she adds, then blushes.

"It's true," Beckett says.

His dick is at half-mast. I don't mean to notice, but it's not like I haven't seen his dick before — how many times have we fucked the same woman? — and it's *right* there.

Fucker.

"Sounds like your favorite kind of literature," I say to Beckett. "Sexy and overwrought."

"Just like my memoir will be," he says, and finally grabs a notebook and pen from the desk behind him.

With a final glance at Bianca, he rises, then walks for the door.

"Enjoy the book," he says, and walks past me.

I turn and follow him back out into the main area of the cabin, where we sit. I read. He doodles or something, and neither of us speak for a very long time.

• • •

Later that day, close to sunset, I take a walk to secure the perimeter. This whole scenario — protecting the princess — has made me jumpy and anxious, constantly looking at every window to see whether a noise was a branch or an assassin.

There's nothing, of course. Nothing looks even *remotely* suspicious: there's the whole stone façade of the cabin, the low wall around it, the massive trees that were probably planted by my great-times-five grandparents.

The only thing out of place is the all-wheel-drive Jeep that we drove here in, an hour down the rutted dirt tracks that are the only way to even *get* here. When the main method of transportation was mules and horses, that didn't matter so much — but now it's at least ideal for keeping Bianca safe from whoever's hunting her.

As I come back around the side of the cabin, I see her, standing on the veranda, leaning against the railing with her arms crossed, looking at the still-covered hot tub.

Even though she's just wearing jeans and a shirt, she's still stunningly beautiful, beyond gorgeous. I stop for a moment just to catch my breath, let myself appreciate the curves of her body, the way her hair flows past her neck and over her shoulders.

Before I can say anything, she turns to look at me.

"You didn't tell me there was a hot tub," she says, tilting her head slightly.

I walk forward, eyes still feasting on her body.

"I didn't know I was supposed to."

"Of course you were supposed to," she says, a smile around her eyes as I get closer. "If you'd told me I'd have brought a swimsuit."

Now I'm on the veranda as well, leaning against a post, only a few feet from Bianca.

"You know," I say. "We're the only ones around for miles and miles. There's no reason you *need* a swimsuit."

"You and Beckett are still here," she says. "Unless you're promising you won't look..."

Her face is totally innocent, but there's *something* in her tone that tells me she knows we will.

That we'll look, and she'll know, and she'll *like* it.

For *easily* the thousandth time I think about the conversation that Beckett and I had last night. About how neither of us will make a move for Bianca, since we know she won't share us. And no hell sounds worse than lying awake in my bed at night, knowing that she's with *him*.

But I'm starting to rethink that position. I've got a feeling that, despite her virginal state, Bianca might not be quite as *innocent* as we've been thinking. Just because she's a virgin doesn't necessarily make her sweet.

After all, every single girl we've ever shared was a virgin once upon a time. Who knows what kind of girl is hiding inside Bianca?

"I don't think I can *promise* that," I say, keeping my

voice low and serious. "If there's a *situation*, we might need to come rescue you."

I try not to imagine it, but I can't stop myself. The way she'd bend over the hot tub to take the cover off, the deep pink edges of her pussy just barely peeking out from between her legs. Her getting into the hot tub, breasts bobbing in the water, nipples puckering among the bubbles.

I wonder if I could hold my breath long enough to eat her pussy and make her come, I think.

Maybe.

"What kind of situation?" she asks, still playful. "I need to know what not to do before I commit to getting naked out here."

"Well, I can't exactly say before it happens, can I?" I say. "The only way to really *know* is to try it out and see if anything can coax us out of the house while you're out here stripped, hot, and wet."

Now she flushes, her cheeks flaming all the way down to her neck, but she doesn't look away from me.

"Who knows?" I say. "I might not take much at all to get us to come."

I leave a long, *long* pause.

"...Out to rescue you," I finish.

Not thinking about it is fucking hopeless. I'm hard as a rock, imagining Bianca standing in front of me, water frothing around us as she grabs the side of the tub, her body buoyed up. The way I could grab her legs and lift her.

Or it could be both of us, her sandwiched between us, half-floating. I could claim her sweet, tight little pussy, her hard, pink nipples rubbing against me as she moaned while Beckett claimed her *other* hole and I watched her eyelids flutter, her brain nearly short-circuiting...

"Sounds like the only way for me to know is to try it," she says, her face still red, but with something *wicked* in her blue eyes.

She wants this, I realize.

She's gonna do it. She's gonna come out here, naked, into this hot tub.

And sweet fucking Jesus, I'm going to have to resist her.

Behind me, the door opens. I know it's Beckett, so I just glance around, pretending to be perfectly casual.

He gives me a long, hard look up and down. There's no way he misses my bulging erection, but right now, I don't even care.

We're even now, I think.

"Want to help me with dinner?" he asks.

I give Bianca one more long, lingering glance, and I swear the girl shudders.

"Think about that offer," I say, and follow Beckett back into the house.

CHAPTER TEN

Bianca

I almost rip my clothes off right then and there, standing on the veranda of Kieran's hunting cabin. He could tell me to do *anything* with that voice and I'd be completely helpless to do anything but obey him.

He heads back into the cabin and I fight the urge, even as I make eye contact with Beckett, too, *his* voice echoing in my ear.

Licking you until you come twice.

Fucking you until you scream my name.

I want it. My pussy is overflowing with juices right now, my knees practically weak. The bad, naughty part of me wants to tear off all my clothes and *run* after them beg them to take me, but I don't.

I *can't*. Because I'm not that girl.

I've never done more than kiss a boy before, and I have no idea how to seduce someone. I don't even know how to pick which of them I *want* to seduce — the charming, sandy-haired Beckett, with the easy smile who teases me?

Or Kieran, who's dark and serious, with that *purr* of a voice that makes me want to fall to my knees?

I can't decide.

I don't know *how* to decide, but I know I'd have to — fantasies aside, having two men at once is just...

...It's *dirty*. It's filthy. It's simply *not done*.

Except it is, a voice in my head whispers.

You know it is.

And you know that no one ever has to know.

I take a deep breath, smooth my hair.

It's just the trauma of being stalked and threatened that's making you feel this way, I tell myself, except I know it's a lie.

How many nights did I lie awake the first time I met them, thinking of Beckett on one side of me, Kieran on the other?

How many times did I pleasure myself thinking of them *sharing* me in the dirtiest, most intimate way possible?

This isn't new, think.

It's not new, and it's not going away.

And no one will ever have to know.

I give my head a quick shake, turn on the hot tub so it can warm up, and then walk inside.

• • •

My hands are shaking as I grab a towel from my bathroom. It's also clearly from a bygone area, though it's in perfectly good shape — it's dotted with pink and green palm trees, along with the purple silhouettes of flamingos.

I don't even wonder why the palm trees are pink and not the flamingos. I'm *that* distracted.

Slowly, in my own bedroom, I take off my shirt and jeans, tossing them both on a chair in the corner. My stomach is in knots, but even *now* I'm so wet that my upper thighs are damp.

I grab a hair tie and pull my hair up so it won't be in the water.

And then I wrap the towel around myself, tuck the corner in, and turn the doorknob.

You could be wrong, I remind myself. *You've never done this before, you could be reading their signals all wrong and you'd have no idea.*

But then I think of having to spend another night here, alone. Quietly getting myself off, trying not to moan their names out loud.

Knowing that they're right next door, but not doing

anything about it.

There's a crazy hacker collective out there, and they want me dead, or dismembered, or disgraced, or *something*. Don't I deserve to have what I want in the meantime?

I push the door open, my heart beating so fast I think it might explode, and I walk through the hallway, toward the kitchen.

The moment I emerge, the conversation that Kieran and Beckett were having melts away into nothingness, and they both *look* at me.

It's not even a look.

They *devour* me with their eyes. I can practically feel them already, hands whispering down my body as they invade my most secret places, whisper *I'm going to lick you and fuck you and lick you again* in my ear.

Despite myself, I shiver, the sensation racing down my spine. The towel's not very big — it covers me from chest to upper thigh, but I'm suddenly wishing that it either covered way, way more or way less.

"Hi," I say. "I was just going to try out the hot tub..."

I trail off, licking my lips. As bold as I was feeling a few moments ago, all my courage is suddenly gone, and I can't even say *don't come out there because I'll be skinny dipping*.

Slowly, Beckett takes a chunk of carrot and pops it

into his mouth.

"Did you bring a swimsuit?" he asks, his gaze slowly raking down my towel-covered body.

Just *that* makes my pussy throb, the way he's *looking* at me like he already knows what's underneath the palm trees and flamingos.

"No," I say, suddenly shy.

"That means don't go out there," Kieran says, shooting Beckett a deadly look before resting his eyes on me again.

Beckett ignores the look.

"Need a hand?" he asks.

Already, I can tell they *both* have erections, their stiff cocks pushing at their pants, straining against zippers. Despite myself, I bite my lip and *stare*.

I've never seen a cock in person before. Sure, I've watched porn — Voravia *does* have the internet — but I've never been close enough to a naked one to touch it.

I'm half a second away from loosening my towel, letting it fall to the floor, and seeing what happens, but I chicken out. Instead I lower my eyes, swallow hard, and walk through the kitchen.

"I'm all right, thanks," I say. "Call me for dinner, and no peeking until I'm in the tub."

"How are we supposed to know when you're in if we don't peek?" Beckett asks, grinning.

Kieran makes a low noise in his throat, and I just scamper through the back door, heading for the hot tub before I can lose my nerve for *that*, too.

It's heated up nicely, and I swish my hand around for a moment before turning the bubbles on, then glance back at the door, still nervous.

It's too light outside for me to see through it well. For all I know they could both be watching me right now, just *waiting* for me to drop this towel.

Or they could be totally immersed in chopping and prepping dinner, already having forgotten about me. I think that's even worse, because after all... don't I *want* them to be watching?

I close my eyes, take a deep breath, and loosen the top of the towel, slowly unwinding it from around myself. I steel myself, then finally whip it off and toss it over the veranda railing, then get into the hot tub as fast as humanly possible, glancing over at the door as the frothy bubbles finally cover me.

Relax, I tell myself. *They can't see you anymore.*

I close my eyes, letting my head sink against the side. I can't shake the image of their erections from my mind, of *both* of them watching me, practically willing my towel off.

I wonder if they can see me at all right now, I think. *Water's clear, even if the bubbles aren't quite. Maybe...*

God, the thought of them *still* watching, their eyes

locked on my form as I relax out here. My skin's getting flushed with the heat of the water, but there's *another* heat blossoming inside my core, this one velvety and molten.

There's a jet against my lower back, and I move my hips slightly, letting it ease the knots there. It feels *good*.

It almost feels like someone massaging me, holding my hips, pressing his thumbs into my spine.

I take another deep breath, eyes closed. My thighs part almost on their own, my fingers skimming over one nipple, just below the surface of the water.

They're not watching, I tell myself. *They're making dinner, they're distracted, they can't see anything anyway. They just think you're relaxing in the tub.*

They'd never come out here, both of them together, one licking your nipples while the other held you against the side of the hot tub and fucked you hard with his enormous cock.

That thought makes a ball of lightning practically explode inside me, just like it does every single time I have it. Before I know it, I'm sighing out loud, one hand pinching my nipple and the other rubbing my clit hard, legs spread wide as my hips move and buck in their own rhythm.

But it's okay, because there's no way they can see me.

CHAPTER ELEVEN
Beckett

I've still got the knife in my hand, dangling by my side. There's a half-chopped carrot on the cutting board, but it may never get chopped. I couldn't care less.

Because we're watching Bianca get herself off in the hot tub.

Right there. In plain fucking view.

We're both watching her, from opposite sides of the kitchen island, both frozen in place, whatever we were doing before completely and utterly forgotten, because this is the sexiest thing I've ever seen. I'm hard as a fucking rock, my dick just about ready to snap in half, and I can *tell* Kieran feels the same way.

"Our agreement didn't factor this in," I say, my voice coming out rough with desire.

"No," he says, his voice sounding far away.

Outside, she gasps, turning her head to one side. Bites her lip, squeezes her eyes shut. I can't see what *exactly* she's doing, but I know what a woman pleasuring herself looks like — I've seen it plenty of times — and I know exactly what she's doing.

"Jesus," I whisper.

"Fuck," Kieran agrees.

I wish I was out there, in the tub with her. I wish it was *me* she was making those noises about, my cock stuffed deep inside her making her sigh and her eyes roll.

I wish I were fucking her up against the side, watching her perfect tits bounce and jiggle, still slick with water as I drove myself into her again and again, her head back.

I glance over at Kieran, and I can tell he's thinking the *exact* same thing. He wants her just as much as I do, but of course, she's an innocent, pure, perfect *virgin* and she'd never go for both of us at once.

Except... she's out there, *right now*, naked and pleasuring herself. She *knows* we're right here. She's got her own bedroom, her own bathroom, *plenty* of places to go do this and she chose being in full view of the two of us.

Bianca throws her head back again, her perfect red lips parted in ecstasy. One nipple comes partly out of the water and I watch her pinch the rosy bud with her fingers, rubbing the wet surface as she sighs.

I could grab her hair, pull her head over the edge and slide my cock between her lips, feel the vibrations as she moans...

Kieran clears his throat, and I realize he's looking at me, the raw hunger, need, and *want* plain on his face.

"That agreement," he says.

I swallow, my mouth dry. On the veranda, Bianca bites her lip like she's trying to stifle a moan.

"Yeah?"

"Only accounted for *one* of us."

I flick my eyes to Kieran, then we both glance back at Bianca, gasping in the hot tub, her face pink, right at the edge of orgasm.

"So what if she *does* want both of us at once, you're saying?"

"Right."

"Kieran," I say, still watching her. "You're on."

As the words come out of my mouth, Bianca comes. Her head goes back, eyes closed, mouth open. She arches her back so hard that both nipples come out of the water, pebbled pink buds against her white skin.

There's a moment where I think I might come in my pants, something I haven't done since I was thirteen. But it's so fucking *sexy*, so perfectly raw, that I nearly can't help myself.

Gradually, Bianca relaxes in the tub. I squeeze the

knife in my hand, remembering that it's there, and turn back to the cutting board, only glancing her way every ten seconds or so. Five minutes pass that way, then ten. We both continue making dinner without speaking, both looking at the glass back door every so often.

It's torture. Total fucking torture to have to *watch* her come without being able to do anything, to not know whether I'll ever get to touch her.

But then she finally opens her eyes again. Her skin has all gone a light shade of pink, like she's finally getting too warm in the hot tub, and she looks up at the sky and sighs.

Glances at the glass door, where Kieran and I are both frozen inside.

Bites her lip. Seems to decide something.

And gets out of the hot tub, her body dripping and shining with moisture. She climbs over the edge gracefully, crosses the two steps to where her towel is, grabs it.

Then sits on the side of the hot tub and dries herself off, starting with her feet. Both of us are fucking spellbound by her beauty, and I want to lick every droplet of water off of her pale skin, flushed pink, taste every inch of her.

Finally, she wraps the towel around herself, tucking the corner in above her breasts. She spends a moment standing there, on the veranda, looking around the cabin at the darkening woods as she pulls a tie out of her hair and shakes out the shining black waves.

Bianca turns the jets off in the hot tub and closes the cover, always conscientious. On the other side of the door, I think I might be dying every moment until she comes back inside.

Bianca pads to the other side of the veranda, looking at something. She comes back, puts her hand on the doorknob, pauses.

My cock feels like it might just *explode* with anticipation.

Then, at least, she opens the door. Kieran and I aren't even pretending that we're still making dinner, we're just standing there, leaning against the counter, drinking in every glorious inch of her. She closes the door softly, then turns to look at us.

"You have a nice time in the hot tub?" I ask, unable to keep a possessive growl out of my voice.

CHAPTER TWELVE

Kieran

Bianca clears her throat, her cheeks flushing even pinker than they already were.

"It's very relaxing," she says, suddenly nervous.

"I believe it," Beckett says, a smirk around his lips. "I'm always more relaxed after I come, too."

Her mouth opens, then closes, then opens again, her hand tight around the closure of the towel, and she glances at me desperately.

"What?" she whispers.

"I said, I'm always more relaxed after I get myself off," Beckett says, a cocky confidence in his voice. "Though the thing I don't understand is... why didn't you ask for help?"

Her eyes flick from him, to me, to him again.

"We *are* here at your beck and call, Princess," I say, leaning back against the kitchen counter. "Anything you might need, we're happy to do for you."

Bianca shoves a hand through her thick, dark hair, taking another deep breath like she's trying to gather her nerve to say something, but keeps faltering.

"Or, if you're having trouble *asking*," Beckett says, sauntering toward her. "We could try offering and you could just say *yes*."

He takes one hand, pulls her into the kitchen, and she trips lightly after him. Somehow, her towel stays on, even as he twirls her once, like they're dancing and stops her as she's facing me, his hands on her shoulders.

Over her head, his eyes are smoldering, flicking up to mine once, then back down to hers, and I understand the meaning exactly.

He's saying *this is our chance.*

This is the only way we can have her.

"For example," I say, stepping forward. "I could help you out of this damp towel."

I place one finger in the hollow of her throat, lower it slowly. Just *touching* her like this sets a shower of sparks off across my skin, every nerve coming alive.

Bianca doesn't answer, but her breathing quickens. Her eyelashes flutter, and Beckett's hands slide down her arms.

"You have to say *yes*," I murmur, getting even closer. "I know you know what you're getting into, Princess."

She gasps, softly, my lips inches from hers. Beckett puts one hand in her hair, sliding his fingers through it, and she tilts her head back slightly.

"One little word," he murmurs, bending closer to her ear, his lips brushing it.

She gasps again.

"Three little letters," he whispers.

Bianca swallows.

Her eyes drift shut.

"Yes," she finally whispers.

I crush my mouth against hers, unable to stop myself. She tastes like cherry lip balm and vanilla and a little like the chlorine of the hot tub as I press harder against her, pushing her lips open with my own, swiping my tongue along her bottom lip.

Bianca moans into my mouth, so quietly I can barely hear it, but the vibrations are unmistakable. I take it as an invitation to slide my tongue past her teeth and find hers, wrestling her, pushing her back against Beckett's thick, hard body.

When I let her go, Bianca's panting for breath, her chest heaving below the towel. Beckett's got a hand in her hair, and he pulls her head to the side, leaning over, claiming her mouth as well.

I flick my finger under the towel, untucking the corner, and it falls around her feet. Bianca gasps and Beckett growls, her white neck long with her head tilted upward, so I bite it.

She makes a *noise*, and at the same time I run my hands up her body, starting at her hips, skimming her warm, slightly damp skin until I'm at her full breasts, her pink nipples between my fingers.

She moans. I bite her neck again, harder this time, squeeze her nipples as I caress them, *anything* to hear that noise. I keep biting, sucking, her skin tasting slightly of chlorine but warm and luscious, just what I'd imagined.

I suck one nipple into my mouth, swirling my tongue around it. I run my teeth over the pebbled surface, and I *want* to bite her, make her cry out in half-pleasure, half-pain, make her gasp and whimper and tangle her hands in my hair, but I don't.

Not *yet*. Even though I can already smell how bad she wants this, her scent pungent in my nose, Bianca's a virgin. Untouched. That sort of thing is for *later*.

"Did it make you wetter knowing we were watching?" Beckett growls.

Now I'm on my knees in front of her, sliding my teeth from a nipple. Her knees go weak for a moment, but Beckett catches her.

I put my hands around her hips, steadying her as

well.

"I didn't think you could see me," she moans, leaning back into him.

I press my lips against her belly, dip my tongue into her bellybutton. Beckett grabs her hand and pulls it behind her.

"Feel that?" he asks as I bite her on the hip. "We were watching every second, Princess. Just like you wanted us to."

I'm panting for breath, my face right in front of her thighs. She's so wet that I can see her juices shining on her upper thighs, trickling down the inside, her scent enrapturing.

"Did knowing we were watching you make you this wet?" I ask her, slipping one finger between her legs, my lips against her mound as I speak. "Did you wish we were fucking you when you came in the hot tub?"

She moans again, whispers something that I'm nearly positive is *yes*.

"Tell me how you get yourself off," I say, my lips still brushing against her.

"With my fingers," she whispers.

I find the soaking wet edges of her lips, tease them. I'm just *barely* brushing against her swollen clit, and she shudders, still sensitive.

"Do you rub this?" I ask, circling one finger around her clit.

My toes curl with the desire to suck it into my mouth, make her pant and moan and *scream*, but I resist.

"Or," Beckett says, his voice rumbling from above. "Do you fuck yourself?"

His hand invades her too, one finger sliding along her swollen, needy pussy.

"Maybe you do both," I suggest.

"Sometimes," she whispers.

It's all either of us need. I flick my tongue out, over her swollen clit, at the same time that Beckett slides one thick finger into her pussy, and Bianca responds like she's been electrified, her body jolting and jerking.

I grab her knee, bend it, push it over my shoulder so I can hold her up and we can both have better access.

"Is this what you thought about when you got yourself off?" Beckett growls, one hand fucking her, the other hand holding her up. "Both of us pleasuring you at the same time, my hand in your pussy and his mouth on your clit?"

I suck her into my mouth, flick my tongue across her lightly. Bianca cries out, grabs my hair, practically shoving my face into her.

Beckett just chuckles. I flick my tongue again.

"That's another *yes*," he says, and I can feel him add another finger to her, just from the ripple it sends through her body.

Now she's panting even harder for breath, her clit throbbing in my mouth, her juices running down Beckett's hand and down my chin. I suck them in, drinking her sweet honey, teasing her right toward the very edge.

Beckett adds one more finger, and with my mouth on her clit I can *feel* how full she is right now. She moans at the sensation, the sound turning into a whimper halfway through. I reach a hand up to her nipples, and I pinch one, Beckett the other.

"Is this how you wanted to come?" he asks her.

I suck harder at her, my tongue flicking faster, Beckett's fingers sunk deep into her pussy.

"Getting shared by the two of us, you dirty girl?"

Bianca just pants, moans. I don't think she can even talk right now.

"We're just getting started, Princess," he growls. "We've *both* thought long and hard about all the ways we're going to fuck you until you scream our names."

He pushes deeper, and I lap at her faster. Her body is tight, taut, like a rubber band about to snap.

"So why don't you come like you want to?" Beckett says, and that's all it takes.

Bianca's hand in my hair clenches, every muscle in her body going rigid as she cries out with her orgasm. It rocks through her body, nearly knocking her over, but I keep licking and sucking at her while she moans and whimpers, desperate to get every last drop of pleasure that I can from the girl right now.

Gradually, her body stops clenching, stops rocking. Her breathing evens out, and after one final swipe at her clit, I move back onto my heels and look up at her, still licking honey off my lips.

"You like being shared, Princess?" I ask.

CHAPTER THIRTEEN
Bianca

Beckett's fingers slide out of me, leaving a thin trail of my juices on my ass, and my body responds with a shock.

I'm leaning back against him, Kieran kneeling in front of me, the two of them still holding me up because I don't think I can move. If I try, I think my muscles might simply all collapse beneath me, and I'd be a naked puddle on the kitchen floor.

Oh my God.

We're in the kitchen. And I'm naked.

Neither of them is naked. But I'm naked.

And I just came super hard.

Somehow, that makes this all even *dirtier*, that I just got coaxed to climax by two fully-clothed men while standing in the kitchen. It makes me feel a little like a sex object.

My pussy twitches, just once.

I'm not sure I mind that feeling, I think.

Not if it's going to feel like that all the time.

"I think she likes it," Beckett says, and I snap halfway back to reality. "She likes it so much she can't even answer."

He's right. All I can do is nod weakly, trying to gather my wits. Beckett kisses my neck again, slowly working his way up to my cheek. I try to turn my head and meet my mouth with his, but I come off balance, and only his strong arms keep me from falling.

Then Kieran's standing in front of me, his dark eyes piercing as ever, but there's something tender in them now, something *different*.

"At least say something," he murmurs.

I swallow, forcing myself together.

"I liked it," I say, and finally, Kieran smiles.

He kisses me. Beckett kisses me, his hands gentle now instead of rough, and Kieran picks up my towel, wraps it gently around my body.

"Go get dressed," he whispers in my ear. "We'll finish dinner."

I blink, then look down. He's got a *massive* erection, his dick tenting up his pants. It's obvious that this isn't over, and I search his eyes with mine.

"But..." I start.

"We've got plenty of time," Beckett says. "Why take things too quickly?"

I bite my lip. I try not to show it, but I'm *disappointed*.

As good as that felt — as *wonderful* as it was — I want... more.

I want more than their fingers and tongues.

I want them to make me *scream*, both fucking me at once until it feels so good I can't control myself any more. I want the stories I've read, the ones that I've fantasized about incessantly almost since the moment I met these two.

"What about you?" I ask, my voice coming out whispery and quiet, not at all how I meant it to.

Kieran smiles, cups my chin in his hand. He still smells like *me*, and that fact just makes me wetter.

"Don't worry," he says, blue eyes glinting. "There's gonna be a round two."

• • •

I head back to my room like I'm floating on air, barely feeling the floor beneath me. I pull on clothes, hardly thinking about it.

I'm blissed-out. I feel like I'm high or drunk or *something*, totally dreamy as I head back into the kitchen, where the two men are still fixing dinner, erections still full-force.

I can't stop staring. My pussy can't stop throbbing, and I can't stop thinking about getting fucked with one of *those*, the way it would fill me harder and deeper than Beckett's fingers.

As I walk to the table, taking a seat, Beckett hands me a glass of red wine.

"Are you trying to get me drunk?" I ask, trying to tease him.

"What purpose would that serve?" he teases right back. "We just fucked you right here in the kitchen and you were perfectly sober."

I blush hard, taking a sip, because even though he's right I can't help it. There's a tiny part of me that can't *believe* I did that.

Even though I'm going to do it again if I get my way.

Lots of times. Lots and *lots*.

"It's a 1994 Côte de Rhone," Kieran volunteers from across the kitchen. "You *could* just enjoy it."

I take the glass, sit at the kitchen table, and watch them finish making dinner. As I drink and the three of us chat, the knot of tension in my chest subsides, and — astonishingly — I start feeling... *normal*.

So what if we all just did that? I think. *It's not that weird.*

We eat dinner, and it somehow feels more and more *normal*. Maybe even better than yesterday, before we'd all had sex, because now I don't feel quite so weird about wanting to have sex with them.

· · ·

When we're done, since the two of them made dinner, I figure it's my turn to clean up. Sure, I grew up in a palace and don't have the very best handle on household chores, but I can figure out how to do some dishes, right?

The moment I'm leaning over the sink, running the hot water, I feel someone come up behind me. Big hands lean on either side of mine, and a huge body — and a massive erection — are pressed against my back.

"What do you think you're doing?" Kieran breathes in my ear.

Instantly, I'm molten. My fingers and toes curl, heat flowing through me like a river, and my pussy thrums and throbs.

"The dishes?" I whisper in response.

"But it's not time to do those yet," my murmurs, his lips right against the shell. "We haven't had dessert yet."

My whole body is flushed and hot, my skin tingling with anticipation.

"That is," he growls. "If you're ready for dessert."

I can only nod as Kieran's hand grabs my hair,

pushing my head forward. His lips briefly travel down my neck, his other hand sneaking up my shirt and finding my breast, pinching my already-stiff nipple.

"Sure feels like you're ready," he says, and before I can answer or even moan, he lifts me off my feet, into his arms, and carries me from the kitchen past a grinning Beckett.

I don't ask where we're going, because I don't ask stupid questions. I *know*.

Moments later, Kieran tosses me onto the bed. I'm wearing short jersey shorts and a t-shirt — panties, no bra. I'm sideways on the bed, and as soon as I land, Kieran's between my knees, his hardness already pressed up against my heat.

Beckett is on the other side of the massive bed, and if I tilt my head back I can see him. He bends over and kisses me deeply, the upside-down sensation strange, and he rubs my stiff nipples through my shirt as he does, making me writhe with pleasure.

While Beckett rubs and tweaks my nipples, shivers coursing through my body, Kieran runs both hands up my thighs, underneath my shorts, and strokes the outside of my panties with one thumb, making me moan into Beckett's mouth.

Kieran's lips are on my belly as he says, "Are you this wet for us?"

I just gasp, nodding.

"Your panties are soaked straight through, Princess," he goes on. "If I didn't know better I'd think you liked being this dirty."

I can't think of a response, but my hands finally find Beckett's pants. It's tricky upside-down, but I manage to unbutton them, pull his zipper down.

Kieran rubs his cock against me, both of us still clothed, and I roll my hips, moaning, as Beckett's cock finally springs free of his pants.

My eyes widen in shock.

That's really big, I think, momentarily stunned.

It's...

"You can touch it, Princess," Beckett growls. "It won't break."

Taking a deep breath, I grab it with one hand and stroke him slowly, carefully. After a moment, Beckett wraps his hand around mine, making me squeeze him much tighter, bringing us both to the thick base of his cock.

"Oh," I gasp.

At the exact same time, Kieran grabs my shorts by the waist, pulls them off completely, and with his other hand Beckett pulls my shirt up and over my nipples. The cool air hits me both places at once, making me shudder and shiver all over.

"Perfect," Kieran growls, his hands making their way up my thighs again. "You're so fucking beautiful,

Bianca."

"Are you ready to become ours?" Beckett growls above me, stroking my hand down his shaft again as he tweaks a nipple.

"Yes," I gasp, and then Kieran slides his fingers into my pussy, reaching them deep.

"Yes!" I nearly scream.

He puts his mouth on my clit, tongue flicking back and forth, fingers bending and twisting inside me. My body bucks and moves of its own accord, back arching as Beckett chuckles above me, my fist still on his cock.

"You like getting fucked, don't you?" he murmurs. "You like the way it feels when he's inside you?"

I can only pant for breath as Kieran adds a third finger, sliding it as far in as it'll go.

"Yes," I whisper, weakly.

Beckett lowers his cock to my mouth. The angle is a little awkward but as Kieran keeps fucking and licking me, I dart my tongue out quickly, lap at the head of Beckett's cock.

Beckett growls again, a drop of precum gathering at his tip. I lick him again, the salt coming off on my tongue, and I swallow the miniscule amount.

I want *more*. Even though I'm half-mad with the pleasure of what Kieran's doing to me, I want *both* of them inside me at once, and I open my mouth further, lick the underside of Beckett's cock from tip to root, moaning as I do.

Kieran swirls his tongue around my clit, and I get closer to the edge. I'm nearly hypnotized by these two men, by having them both at the same time, all to myself.

"Make me come again," I beg. "Please."

Just instead of licking me harder, Kieran stops. He pulls out, moves his mouth away, back up my belly, and he licks one nipple, then the other.

"Not that way," he murmurs. "We've been waiting for this for weeks, Princess, and we both want to be inside you this time."

I gasp, my eyes flying open, hand still on Beckett's shaft.

"That's not—" I stammer. "I mean, I can't, I've never even—"

Kieran laughs. He bites one nipple a little harder, sucking at it, turning my protest into a moan.

Then he lets go, moves back, and in one deft movement, together they flip me over onto my stomach and I yelp.

I hear clothing hit the floor, and when Kieran's between my legs again, he's suddenly bare, the two of us skin-to-skin. I struggle to my hands and knees, then watch Beckett as he takes his clothes off too, his hard, sculpted body rippling in the low light.

Kieran puts his fingers to my clit again, slides them

up my wetness to my slit, pushes then inside me briefly as I moan, grabbing Beckett's cock with my fist again.

Then he keeps going, circling my tight back hole with my own wetness. My eyes go wide, my toes curling, my whole body tensing.

"Not *these* two holes," he says, almost teasing me as his fingers circle me, again and again. "Not tonight, at least."

Beckett grabs my thick black hair in his fist, tilting my head back so I can look up at him.

"We're not monsters," he says, his voice rumbling in his chest. "Just two men desperate to fuck you at the same time."

Just then, I feel Kieran's cock nudge apart my lower lips. I whimper with need, eyes closed, as Beckett keeps my head back.

"Look at me while he fucks you," Beckett says, and my eyes pop open. Kieran's cock pushes against my slick, wet entrance and I bite my lip, even as my eyelids threaten to slide shut.

Kieran's thumbs stroke my swollen lips, one on either side of his thick head, and I don't break my gaze with Beckett.

Slowly, he pushes himself inside me, so gradually I think I can feel every millimeter of his massive cock as my swollen, needy pussy stretches around him and a shaky sigh escapes my lips.

Behind me, Kieran groans, and I see something flick across Beckett's handsome face even as my eyelids are flickering, my breath coming fast and hard.

"You're fucking tight, Princess," Kieran growls, both his hands on my hips as he sinks himself into me, bit by bit. "Your pussy's like a glove."

I moan, teeth between my lips, still looking up at Beckett. Suddenly Kieran slides in a little further, changing the angle slightly, and I inhale sharply, eyes rolling.

"There's the spot," Kieran growls. "You like it when I fuck you there, Princess?"

He does it again, and my entire body clenches with pleasure.

Beckett takes my chin in his other hand, runs his thumb over my bottom lip, his face still careful.

"He asked you a question," he rumbles. "You like getting fucked?"

"Yes," I whisper, pushing backward on my hands and knees, unable to stop myself. "Don't stop, *please*."

The next thing I feel is Kieran's hips against my ass, my pussy tightening around him. Beckett pulls a little harder on my hair, his thumb still on my lip, his eyes half on my face, half on Kieran as he fucks me.

I feel impossibly stretched, filled up totally and completely. It hurts a little, but much more than that is the overwhelming *pleasure* of having Kieran's entire cock inside me at once, and I pull forward slowly, a little unsteady.

This time he fucks me harder when he fucks me, his entire cock sinking into me with a single stroke, and I cry out with pleasure, my hands knotted in fists on the bedspread.

Beckett runs his thumb over my bottom lip again, then pushes it into my mouth, only I suddenly realize it's *not* his thumb.

I open wide, accepting his cock between my lips, licking and sucking at the thick head as Kieran fucks me, Beckett's hand still in my hair.

Slowly, I rock back and forth between the two men. With every back stroke I take more of Kieran, moaning into Beckett's cock with pleasure, and on every forward stroke I push my lips down Beckett's shaft.

Soon, I'm moving faster, a little less awkwardly, licking and slurping at Beckett, listening to him moan and growl, hearing Kieran's breathing get faster and faster.

It's fucking *incredible*, taking both of them at once. It's everything I thought it would be and more, even as my eyes are watering and Beckett is grabbing my hair, growling at me.

"You're so fucking pretty with my cock in your mouth," he growls. "And you're even prettier when he fucks you from behind."

"You're our dirty girl," Kieran says, his voice labored. "You know that there's a spot deep inside your cunt that makes your whole *body* throb when I hit it just right with my cock?"

Suddenly, they both thrust in at once, changing the rhythm, mouth and pussy both totally filled. I look up at Beckett, eyes streaming with tears, but despite that, there's *nothing* I'd rather be doing.

Kieran's cock hits *that* spot again, my whole body shaking with the tremors. I'm *so* close, every nerve in my body alight and on fire.

"Come with us inside you," Beckett orders, his voice rough. "We *both* want to feel you when you hit that climax."

They fuck me again, driving me even closer, pussy drooling around Kieran, greedily shoving my mouth down Beckett's cock because I want *them* too, I want to feel them both come inside me, hard and furious.

They do it again and again, and then suddenly I'm spinning right at that edge and tilting over it, plunging off into the abyss. I moan around Beckett's cock, feel Kieran grip my hips even harder as my pussy clenches around him.

"God, you feel so good," Kieran gasps. "Just fucking *perfect*."

I'm still shaking and gasping, the climax still rolling through me like an earthquake, my elbows close to giving out and dumping me onto the bed.

But I *want* this, want to feel and taste them, so I take Beckett into my mouth, sucking as hard as I can, my whole body begging for him to give me this.

Behind me, Kieran growls, and then I can feel him shudder and *come*, his cock jolting again and again inside me as Beckett holds my hair in his fist, pushing himself against the back of my mouth, unrelenting.

He gasps, teeth clenched, and then he comes in a hard torrent, and I swallow again and again, his salty-sweet liquid flowing down my throat at the same time as Kieran empties himself in my pussy.

I keep sucking Beckett until he pulls out, sucking and licking his cock as he pulls it from my mouth. Kieran pulls out, too, and I can feel his sticky fluid run down the inside of my thigh.

Beckett takes me by the shoulders, pulls me up gently, and together they lift me to kneeling. I feel like I'm made of leaves and twigs, like I might blow away at any moment if they're not careful, but they are. Beckett holds my hips and Kieran takes me around the shoulders, both pressing their lips to me reverently.

As if they didn't just fuck me like the dirty girl I am now.

As if I'm to be treasured, cherished.

"How was your first time?" Beckett asks, his voice a gentle whisper.

I can only nod, words leaving me entirely. Kieran kisses the back of my neck, my shoulder.

"That was fucking perfect, Princess," he whispers.

"Completely fucking perfect," Beckett echoes, and he kisses me gently but deeply, his tongue exploring every crevice of my mouth while Kieran holds me from behind, my heart completely and utterly full.

CHAPTER FOURTEEN

Beckett

I wake up the next morning with Bianca's hair still tangled in my fingers. I'm on one side of her and Kieran's on the other, both of us curled protectively around her.

And strangely, it doesn't feel bad. When I see her nestle into the hollow of his neck, her back warm against me, I'm not jealous.

Instead I'm... *happy*. Happy that the person I trust most in the world is the one on the other side of Bianca. I'm happy that we're *both* here for, that we *both* want to keep her safe.

After a little while, Bianca wakes up too. She yawns, stretches, her warm supple body brushing against mine. On her other side, Kieran mutters something, also coming awake slowly.

Even when we were back in the army together, he could be hard to rouse. Not as hard for a civilian, obviously, but hard for a soldier.

In bed, with Bianca's warm, naked body against me, I hold my breath. I'm hard already — morning wood — but having her right here, lithe and warm and fuckable, isn't doing me any favors. Every time she moves, her ass rubs against my cock, and I've got one hand on her hip.

I'm not pulling her back against me, but I *could.* I'm not sliding my hand between her legs, biting her on the neck, and fucking her sweet wetness from behind before either of us is really awake, but I *could.*

"Morning," I hear Kieran mutter.

"Morning," Bianca murmurs back, then turns her head, rolling partway over and looking at me.

"Good morning," she says again, her voice and eyes sleepy.

Now I grab her hip a little harder, pull her back against me a little more, so I can kiss her on her perfect red mouth, taste her once more. My hard, thick cock is already between her buttocks, and as we kiss harder and deeper and longer, I can feel her arch against me, like her whole body is begging for something.

Suddenly Bianca's mouth comes open and she gasps, her fingers tangling in my hair. On her other side, I can just barely see Kieran's hand on her breast, one rosy nipple between his fingers.

"I'd offer to wake you up, but you seem pretty awake already," he says, a wolfish grin on his face.

Bianca just smiles and laughs softly, lying there between us.

"What kind of wake up did you have in mind?" she asks, tracing her finger down Kieran's hard chest as I watch over her shoulder.

She goes lower and lower, her finger in his furry treasure trail now, until finally she's right as his dick, sliding her hand around it in a tight fist. Just like I showed her last night.

As she does, I grab her hip in my hand even harder, pull her back against me, pressing my own massive, hard cock into her flesh as Kieran groans.

"It hasn't even been twelve hours, you sweet dirty thing," I whisper into her ear.

"Is there a time limit?" Bianca murmurs, her voice already breathless.

"Not for you," I say, gently taking the shell of her ear in my teeth. "*You* can just say the word and we'll be at the ready in seconds, Princess."

I thrust against her shallowly, just to punctuate my point, and I can hear her breathing go ragged. Kieran pinches both her nipples at once, and now she *moans*, her voice breathy and barely awake but beautiful.

That's enough for me. I slide my hands between her legs, up her thighs, until I reach her wet heat, gently taking her clit between two fingers. She's already slick, still moaning, her back arching harder, like her body is begging to be fucked.

"You're already dripping wet," I say into her ear. "What did you dream about, Princess?"

"Was it us? You can tell us," Kieran adds.

I grab my cock, guide the tip to her entrance. I'm so aroused I can barely breathe, my entire being suddenly focused into my shaft, about to slide inside Bianca for the first time.

She doesn't answer the question, just moans again. Kieran ducks his head to her nipples, and I whisper into her ear again.

"Was it having my cock inside you again that you dreamed about? Did you dream I fucked you slow and hard until you came, and then you woke up wet, hoping it would happen?"

"Maybe," she whimpers.

"Then it's your lucky day," I growl. "Because some wishes *do* come true."

Bianca cries out as I slide inside her with a single hard stroke, filing her completely as her near-virgin pussy stretches around me, her muscles all contracting at once.

"Now you've had both of us," I say into her ear.

"Jesus, Bianca, you're tight as fuck and you feel *good*."

"Don't stop," she whispers.

I don't stop. I don't think I *could*, not for all the money in the world, I just dig my fingers into her hip and fuck her as deep and hard as I can, listening to her cry out and moan, back arching, her hands on Kieran's cock while he licks her nipples.

"It feels so good," Bianca moans. "I didn't think it would..."

I pull her hair back just a little, the glorious thick black strands wrapped around my fist.

"Surprise," I whisper into her ear, thrusting as deep as I possibly can. "Turns out you scream hard and come harder with my cock deep inside you."

She writhes, her muscles fluttering, and even though I'm holding onto her as hard as I can, I'm losing my grip because this is a good angle for gentle, morning lovemaking but a bad angle for *fucking*, and the former's become the latter.

I grab her hard, slam back into her, and let go of her hair. In one swift motion I roll onto my side, lifting her in front of me, and Bianca yelps as suddenly she's straddling me in reverse cowgirl, looking back at me in surprise.

I wink at her. She folds her legs underneath her, grabbing my knees, and then she starts riding me.

It takes her a few moments, because she's awkward

at first, not quite sure how to move her body, but then I hit *that* spot inside her and everything changes. She moans and rocks back and forth, rolling her hips, pushing herself up and down on my cock like she can't get enough, moving fast and hard and like she *needs* something I can give her.

Then Kieran's there, too, upright on his knees over my legs, and instantly Bianca's hands are on his hips, stroking his cock, even as she bounces and rides and moans.

I grab her hips and pull her down, stilling her. Kieran pushes his big hand into her hair, both her hands around the root of his cock, and she leans forward. I can't see what happens but from the way he *groans*, from the way her pussy clenches tight around me, I know she's sucking his cock.

Fuck, it's incredible. Kieran growls low, his eyes sliding closed, his fist in her hair as he guides her back and forth, her hands splayed on his thighs. I can *hear* her slurping and sucking him, leaning forward and taking Kieran into her mouth as she lets me slide out of her pussy, slow and sticky and perfectly torturous.

It's the best thing I've ever woken up to, Bianca stuffed full of my cock while Kieran kneels in front of her. Her muscles are already fluttering and clenching around me, moans rising from her throat as her movements get faster, harder. Soon she's slamming down onto me, sinking her tight little body onto me with her full weight with every stroke and I'm gritting my teeth, forcing myself not to release myself into her *yet*.

"That's a pretty fucking sight," Kieran growls.

"Come for us again, Bianca," I gasp. "I can't watch you like this much longer."

She pushes herself down onto me again and I go *deep*, grunting and growling in response, my pure animal instincts engaged, and she tightens around me *hard*, the ring of muscle gripping me like a fist.

I shout. Bianca clenches again, her moan muffled by Kieran's cock, and then she's whimpering and fucking me faster and harder, her pussy fluttering and clenching and milking my cock while she rides me.

"Fuck me like you *need* it," I growl, and by God, she does.

I come in a rush, grabbing her hips so hard I'm sure she'll have bruises. Kieran's knuckles in her hair go white and he pushes her face down onto him, as intense as I've ever seen him.

I think I may never stop coming, emptying spurt after spurt into Bianca as she swallows and swallows, Kieran coming just as hard into her mouth while she rocks back and forth, getting every last ounce of pleasure from us that she possibly can.

After a moment, she slurps Kieran from her mouth,

and he bends down, kisses her on the mouth, my hands tracing gently down her back, caressing the spots where I may have bruised her just a moment ago. She rolls off me, a little ungracefully, then the three of us crawl back into position in her bed, and now it's my turn to kiss her while she snuggles me.

"You still need coffee, or was that enough to wake you up?" I ask.

She laughs and wrinkles her nose.

"I could still use some coffee, I think," she admits.

"Your wish is our command, Princess," I answer her.

CHAPTER FIFTEEN

Aurora

For days, things go on the same way. Just the three of us, in my family's hunting cabin, eating together and drinking together, reading tedious Griskoldian history books, watching the windows for dangerous robot squirrels.

I think I'm losing my mind. I can't think. I can barely breathe, and I'm pretty sure I can't open my eyes, but I don't care because all of this feels incredible, like I'm being swept out to sea by a riptide, but I don't care.

Every muscle in my body is tense, and I can tell that something is about to happen, that I'm building toward a huge explosion, but every time I get close, Declan backs off. He slows down, moves his amazing tongue in circles around my clit, but he never gets me there, always stopping just before it happens.

At least, I think that's what's going on. What if he's really doing the same thing, but I can't come?

"Please," I moan, his tongue on me again, lapping at my clit. "God, Declan, please."

He goes faster, his breath hot on my pussy, and I'm driven irresistibly upward, circling higher and higher. My back arches, and despite myself, I grab his hair in my hands.

"Please," I whimper, but his tongue slows to a crawl.

I can breathe again, but I still haven't reached that peak. I'm so frustrated I could almost cry, but then I feel something else. It's his rough fingers, stroking my lips, parting them.

His tongue still moving, Declan slides one finger inside me. Instantly, he hits that spot, the digit moving inside me, and I gasp for air.

"Oh my God, Declan," I whimper. "Declan, that feels so good, please don't stop. Please."

He doesn't but he moves with torturous, glacial slowness, slowly sliding a second finger in, stretching me gently, moving them together.

No one has ever done this to me before. Any of it. I've been kissed, and that's it, and I know that this is dirty and I shouldn't be doing it, but I can't stop.

"More," I gasp.

I think he chuckles, but I can't tell. I roll my hips insistently, still desperate with desire. All I want is for him to fuck me with one more finger, find that spot inside me, fill me up and stretch me out.

And I want Declan to make me come, finally push me over that edge. I don't even care how he does it — it's what I need.

"Please, Declan," I moan again, my hands tight on the sheets. "Please."

But he doesn't do what I want, and instead, his tongue slows to lazy circles around my clit, close but not touching me, deliberate torture. I'm gasping for air, legs spread wide, completely open to him and at his mercy.

Slowly, he adds another finger. I bite my lip, gasping with pleasure, feeling my tight pussy stretch around him, reveling in the sensation. He twists his hand inside me, and for a split second there's a pinch of pain, but then only pleasure.

Gradually, he licks at me again, his fingers moving in the same rhythm.

Now he's going to make me come, I think. At last.

I can't believe I doubted that he could, but I never thought I'd be here, in this position — completely at Declan's mercy, desperate for his touch, moaning his name and begging him for release.

Declan adds a third finger. My toes curl, and I throw my head back, arching off the bed as I whimper.

I'm walking a tightrope right now, and with the slightest movement I'll finally fall off, have that first, blissful orgasm, but I don't. Declan knows exactly what I'm doing, and even though I'm easily in his power right now, he doesn't let me come.

Even though I want it, desperately, Declan doesn't let me come.

Suddenly, he stops. He pulls his fingers out and kneels over me, still totally clothed, his eyes boring into mine with an intensity I can barely fathom.

Then, he holds his fingers out to me, touching my lips with my own juices.

I'm wide-eyed, astonished, because I don't know what's going on.

Is this a normal part of sex? Is this what happens?

"Lick me clean," he orders, his voice low and commanding.

I can smell my powerful arousal on his fingers, and even though I'm unsure about this, I can't refuse Declan. Not now, my whole body buzzing and humming. Not when every desire I have is concentrated into his form.

"Be a good girl," he whispers, and I open my mouth.

Declan pushes his fingers inside my mouth, all at

once, and the taste of myself is almost overwhelming. I suck on his fingers, licking them, swallowing my own salty-sweet juices again and again.

I can't believe I'm doing this, I think. I can't believe he's talking to me this way, I can't believe...

But I like it. Licking myself from his fingers, following his commands, I'm impossibly turned on. I think the slightest touch might send me straight over the edge and into bliss, so I lick and suck greedily, making sure to get every last sticky drop from him.

Finally, he takes his fingers from my mouth, still wet, and slides them down my body, tracing around one nipple and then the other. I can see his massive erection tenting up the suit pants he's still wearing, and the sight of it makes me half aroused, half afraid.

Declan watches me hungrily, like I'm a steak and he's a starving man, like he's going to take his time savoring me. Slowly, he unbuttons his shirt, revealing a hard sculpted chest, pecs, and abs rippling in the moonlight.

I hold my breath, reaching out to touch him, my fingers moving slowly over the perfection of his body, pussy practically drooling with wetness. They land on the button of his pants, and I look at him, suddenly unsure.

But Declan just laughs.

"Go ahead, Princess," he says, his voice low.

I unbutton his pants, unzip them, and suddenly his enormous cock springs out and I gasp. Declan takes me by the wrist and guides my hand to it, wrapping my fingers around the impossibly thick shaft.

"Oh," I breathe.

I've never touched a penis before. I've never even seen one in person, but this is... nice.

Very nice. His cock fills my whole fist, hard as a steel rod, and as I stroke it he groans, bending over me, pushing my knees over his shoulders.

"It feels so good to finally have you touch my cock, Princess," he murmurs into my ear. "Tell me what else you want me to do with it."

Fuck me, I think, surprising even myself. I want you to fuck me with this as hard as you can.

"Make me come," I whisper, unable to actually express my thought. "Please, Declan, I want you to make me come."

He groans again, pushing his shaft through my hand, the tip brushing against my belly.

"How?" he growls.

"With this," I whisper. "I want you to..."

I can't. I can't. I want to, but I can't bring myself to say the words fuck me out loud.

"Beg me," he murmurs.

CHAPTER SIXTEEN

Bianca

Kieran disappears almost silently. One moment here's there, frowning at the bag of apples in my hand, and the next moment he's gone.

Beckett and I look at each other. I have no idea what's going on, but Beckett's eyes flick warily from my face, to the spot where Kieran disappeared, to the back of the store.

That makes me nervous.

'What is it?" I ask, the bag suddenly tight in my hand.

"Probably nothing, but I'm not sure," he says, voice tense. "I think..."

I raise my eyebrows, waiting for an answer. His lips form a line and he frowns, the spot between his eyebrows just barely creasing.

"I've got a bad feeling," he says, voice low and serious as he takes my hand. "Come on."

I put the apples down and let Beckett lead me back into the sunlit cobblestone street, heart pounding. I don't know what Kieran saw or what Beckett saw, but it was something that put them both on edge, and that means I'm on edge.

"You know how he is," Beckett says, one hand on my shoulder. "He's jumpy, especially when he's on a mission like this, I'm sure someone just looked at him funny and now he's on the hunt—"

Suddenly, there's a huge crash behind me, glass breaking, something heavy smashing. A woman screams, and it's not just a scream of surprise, it's a scream of pain and *terror*.

I can feel the blood drain from my face, and Beckett grabs me, pushes me up against the warm stone wall in the bright sunlight.

"Don't move," he says. "Stay where everyone can see you, I'll be back in a second."

I open my mouth to say *no, don't, what if it's a trap* but then he's gone, jogging around the corner, his whole body rigid and military. It would be sexy as hell if I weren't so *nervous*.

Standing there, against the wall, I take a deep breath. It's so bright, beautiful, and sunny that it's a little hard to stay *this* nervous, be *this* freaked out.

I mean, who'd try something in broad daylight, in full view of a dozen people?

Well, who'd broadcast something during primetime on a national network?

I have a point.

I take another deep breath, collecting myself, my back and shoulders still against the wall. Beckett hasn't reappeared from the alley, and Kieran hasn't reappeared from the shop, but I crane my neck, looking for either of them.

I don't find them.

But I find a dark, hooded figure in a cape. I jump about a mile when I see him, and then a cold shock goes through me, because *he doesn't move*. He didn't move, not at all.

He's been standing there, across the street, in the shadow of an ironwork balcony the whole time. He could have been there for hours, he might have watched me go into the store, pick out apples, come out and—

He grins, his mouth oddly white in the dark shadow, even from this far away.

My whole body breaks into a cold sweat. I don't know who it is or what's happening. For all I know, he could be part of some animatronic Halloween decoration, only it's not October. I just know that he's staring at me, watching me, and grinning in a way that makes my blood run cold.

And then he lifts one hand in a wave, his unnerving grin plastered onto his face.

I start walking. I know that Beckett told me to stay right there and not move, but he's not here. He's not watching this creep in a cloak wave and grin at me, he's not here to go tell him to knock it off or find out what's going on.

And you know what? I've seen horror movies before. I know what happens to the girl who just stands still and screams while the bad guy comes for her.

She dies first. That's what.

No thanks.

I walk as fast as I can along the cobblestone street, my summer dress swishing along my thighs. Even though it's warm I can feel cold prickles along the back of my neck, the ooze of cold sweat trickling down my body.

He's coming, I think. *He's watching you, and he's walking after you.*

Don't turn around. Don't look. Don't let him know you're afraid, just act normal.

I last another fifteen seconds, and then I can't help it. I turn around and look.

There he is, half a block behind me. His creepy cape is billowing out behind him, lined with blood-red satin, his face deep in shadow under the hood. I can tell he's wearing a full tuxedo despite the summer heat, along with white gloves, walking swiftly. Purposefully.

He's coming for me. There's no other interpretation of this I can make, nothing else I can think.

I gasp, try to get a hold of myself, my hands balled into tight fists at my sides as I push myself to walk even faster down this street, even though I don't know where I'm going. Inversberg is tiny, only a few blocks long, and already the houses and shops are spacing out, but I can't turn back.

He's back there.

I look again, despite myself, and this time he's closer. Still marching steadily for me, and I'm almost out of town, nearly to the dark woods that surround the place.

Go somewhere, I think. *Do something, only don't go back, do something smart and clever and outwit him somehow...*

Up ahead, I can see one last shop, the door open, a chalkboard sign out front that says 'Lose yourself in a book!'

There, I think. *Go in there, call for help, people who like books are always good people.*

Despite myself, I break into a run, but I can hear footsteps behind me, *way* too close. The bookstore is only a block away, and I put every ounce of effort and energy I've got into sprinting for it, completely panicked, every alarm bell in my body blaring at full volume.

Fifty feet. Twenty, ten, and then I'm there next to the cheery chalkboard sign, wrenching open the door so hard that the bells on it slam against the wood.

"Hi, welcome to Isabelle's—"

"Please help me I'm being chased he's right behind me call someone *please*," I gasp, nearly running into a table filled with kids' books.

I dart around it wildly, heading for the counter in the back of the store where there's got to be a phone as I hear the bells on the door again.

He's right behind me, he's right—

"Günther!" a woman's voice says sharply.

I rush between two bookshelves, careening toward the counter. There's no one behind it right now, and I scramble around it, frantically looking for a phone.

Somewhere in there, I look up, toward the front of the store, and I come to a dead stop.

The guy in the cloak is just standing there, hood off, head down, shoulders slumped. The woman who told me hello is standing in front of him, about a foot shorter but *clearly* in control.

"You *know* better!" she says.

"I forgot," he mutters.

I stand up straighter, hands on the counter.

"You can't just *forget*," she warns. "You promised

everyone that would wouldn't play Dracula with strangers, and now here you are, and that poor girl is terrified out of her wits!"

I bristle at that. I'm not some poor girl, and I'm not terrified out of my...

Well. I did kinda freak out there.

"I'm sorry," he mutters. "I thought she was..."

The woman crosses her arms.

"Are you lying?" she asks, her voice still stern.

"I thought she was Rosalind?"

"Günther."

"Maria?"

"You didn't think she was anyone, you just wanted to scare her, and you *know* you broke your promise."

"Sorry, Belle," he whispers.

The woman sighs.

"Sit down," she says. "I'm going to call your grandpa to come get you."

Günther slumps off, and Belle turns authoritatively, walking toward me.

"Hi, I'm *so* sorry about that, he's totally harmless but I know he really scares people," she says, walking toward me. "Are you okay? Can I make you tea or anything? I'm Isabelle, by the way."

Up close, she's prettier and younger than I thought she'd be: honey-brown hair, warm brown eyes, the kind of welcoming smile that makes me feel a little better.

"I'm fine," I say, still catching my breath. "Is that— does he—"

She leans in, confidentially, her eyes looking sad.

"He fell out of a tree as a kid," she says, voice hushed. "Doctors didn't think he'd live, but when he finally woke up there was... *damage*."

"I see."

"Right now, he's really into vampires, and he's invented this game where he stalks people around town, pretending like he's lurking in the shadows, and everyone who lives here knows him and kind of ignores it. Some people even gave him the costume because, you know, *poor Günther*. Six months ago he wanted to be a ballerina, and was always pirouetting into bookshelves."

I move around the counter and sneak a glance of the guy in the cloak. Sitting there, head and shoulders slumped, messing with his fingers, he's not scary at all.

"Right," I say, still trying to collect myself.

Isabelle cocks her head.

"Let me call his grandfather to come get him, then I'll make you some tea, all right?" she says.

CHAPTER SEVENTEEN
Beckett

"HOW COULD YOU FUCKING LOSE HER?" Kieran roars.

"I was gone for fifteen seconds to investigate—"

"You don't fucking leave her, you sock-headed moron!" he shouts. "That was a fucking distraction, a goddamn trap!"

He's right. Jesus, I know he's right, the knowledge burning its way through my chest in a fiery flood as we stand in the middle of this street, shouting at each other. There's a small ring of people around us, all a good twenty feet away, just *waiting* to see what happens next

"I evaluated the surroundings and felt that my attention was best spent elsewhere," I growl through

122

gritted teeth. "Maybe if we focused on finding where she went rather than figuring out whose fault this is—"

"*Yours*," he grits back, jabbing one finger into my chest. "This is *your* fault, you blithering—"

I grab his finger, jerk his hand away from me.

"We can *fucking* do this part later," I snarl. "I'm gonna go find Bianca. You coming?"

Kieran steps back, glaring, and I turn on my heel, striding down the street.

We check the doors on both sides, townspeople pointing us on, my blood still boiling, nerves writhing. As we make our way through town I'm more and more nervous, less and less angry at Kieran.

He's right, I think, over and over again.

I should never have let her out of my sight, that's the oldest trick in the book.

What if she's gone forever? What if I never see Bianca again? What if...

"Clear," Kieran calls from the opposite side of the street, his voice grim.

"Clear," I answer back.

The forest is looming close, right at the edge of town, and the fact is weighing heavily in my gut. We've only spent a few minutes looking for her in town, but what if it was too long?

They could be miles away by now, I think, my hands

balling into fists. *We should just sound the alarm and go, not bother checking this last store...*

But Kieran's already crossing the street, scowl etched on his face, so I walk toward the cheerful chalkboard sign on Isabelle's Bookstore, heave the door open, and peer in.

Sitting in a chair, a head snaps up, and I frown. The guy's wearing a black cloak lined with blood-red satin, but he can't be more than nineteen or twenty, and he's got the open, guileless face of a child.

"Have you seen a woman?" I ask, somehow unnerved by the scene.

He nods, and I realize he's also wearing a tuxedo. The fact only unnerves me more.

"Belle's here," he offers. "She's a woman. And there was the pretty girl who..."

"Beckett?" Bianca's voice asks.

My knees nearly go weak with relief as she suddenly appears between two bookshelves.

I don't say anything, just stride toward her and wrap my arms around her slight frame, hugging her so tight that I'm not sure she can breathe.

"I'm sorry," she gasps out. "He was chasing me, and I just got so freaked out that I—"

"It's fine," I murmur, my lips against her hair. "I should have never left you there alone, I shouldn't have let myself get distracted, it's completely my fault."

The bells on the door ring behind me, and I turn my head to see Kieran come through. The instant that he sees Bianca in my arms, his face changes completely, from worried anger to total relief.

Wordlessly, I let her go and she goes to him, letting him envelop her in his arms.

"I'm fine," I hear her whisper. "I was about to come look for you, but I wasn't sure where you'd be..."

The other woman in the store is just watching the three of us, face slightly amused, arms crossed in front of her chest. She's pretty, brown eyes and brown hair, kind of a bookish look about her. When she sees me looking at her, she raises her eyebrows and walks over to me.

"I'm so sorry about that," she says. "The guy in the cape is Günther, he had an accident as a child and right now he's obsessed with thinking he's a vampire. I swear he's not dangerous, it's just this game he likes to play. When he catches you he just laughs and then goes to catch someone else, I swear. But I know it's easy to get freaked out by a guy in a cape chasing you..."

I look over at Günther, and I feel a little bad for the guy. That does explain the look of childlike confusion on his face, or why someone is wearing a tuxedo and cape in the middle of town at all.

"Thanks for letting her in," I tell the woman.

"Of course," she says.

Bianca and Kieran finally separate, and then the three of us just look at each other.

Then we look at the woman who owns the bookstore, who's *very slightly* raising one eyebrow.

"Oh, Belle, these are my... friends," Bianca says, in a way that makes it clear that *friends* is not at all the right word. "Kieran and Beckett."

Belle clearly doesn't believe the *friends* bit, but she shakes our hands very pleasantly anyway.

"Well, now that you're here, feel free to look around," she says. "This vampire should be out of here shortly, I've called his grandpa to come fetch him."

In his chair, Günther sighs.

• • •

Fifteen minutes later, Kieran and I are both waiting at the counter with huge stacks of books. Probably at least a few hundred euros' worth — it's the least we can do for the woman who helped Bianca out.

As Belle rings us up, I peruse the books on a table behind us. It seems to be the political area.

And it's very... *opinionated*, with titles like *Why Griskold Doesn't Need a Monarchy* or *Viva La Parliament!*

I shrug to myself. It's always good to have a lively discussion about how we're governed.

But then one *more* catches my eye.

The Hidden Beast in the Tower: Why Julian of Griskold Should Not Be the Next King.

I bristle. Not just at the suggestion that Julian wouldn't make an excellent king — he made a fucking good commander, after all — but at the *beast* moniker.

The man's got some issues. Fighting in Griskold's military — *serving his country* — left him a little fucked up, sure. We all have mental scars from it — it just so happens that his are physical, too, and that means his public appearances are rarer than a polar bear in the Sahara.

But that doesn't mean he wouldn't be a good king.

"What's with the anti-Prince-Julian nonsense?" I growl at Belle.

She raises one eyebrow as she scans a book.

"You disagree?" she says coolly.

"I think that refusing to be constantly in front of the cameras doesn't disqualify you from being king."

"But the King of Griskold is our representative to the world," she says. "And if he refuses to fill that role..."

"That role can be filled in lots of ways," Kieran suddenly adds, glancing over his shoulder at the book, his face darkening again. "You don't need to call a solider and patriot a beast."

Belle laughs. I frown, taken aback, as she scans the last book.

"I don't actually agree with that one," she says. "I think Lamont rests far too much of his case against the monarchy on hearsay and rumor, and I agree that it's rude to call the Prince a *beast*. It's just there to rile people up, and riled up people buy books."

Kieran and I exchange a glance. Beside me, Bianca's grinning.

"So it worked," Kieran says.

Belle just shrugs, still smiling.

"Are you riled up?"

I sigh.

"*And* buying books," I say.

"Three forty-five sixty-seven," Belle says.

CHAPTER EIGHTEEN

Kieran

We go straight from Belle's bookshop to the Jeep, waiting on a side street for us. Beckett and I make Bianca wait a few feet away while we quickly check it for explosives, then all climb in. Beckett drives, Bianca rides shotgun, and I sit in the back.

As we leave town and get back on the narrow, rutted road that leads to the hunting cabin, I'm still keyed up. Even though the threat turned out to be nothing at all, it still left an unpleasant taste in my mouth.

Now I know how easy it would be to *actually* steal her away, and the thought makes my blood run cold.

In the rearview mirror, I see Beckett make a face at me. I scowl back, still lost in thought.

"Nothing happened," he points out.

"I know," I mutter.

We're on the dirt road, all three of us slightly jostled as Beckett drives up it, a little faster than I'd like, but I don't say anything. I'd probably be driving hell-for-leather right now too, just to get her back to the safe cabin where I know the doors lock properly.

Sitting in the front seat, Bianca turns toward me. She slides the seat all the way back, lets it down a little.

"I'm sorry," she says, her big eyes wide. "Please don't blame Beckett, it's not his fault, I just saw that guy standing there while I was alone, and... I freaked."

We go over a big bump in the road, and despite myself — despite the *danger* still rattling through my veins — I watch the way her tits bounce under her dress, her nipples half-hard against the fabric.

I look back at her face, and now she's smiling, her smile a little wicked.

"You're not trained in any of this," I mutter. "You're a civilian, you can't be expected to..."

She's still grinning wickedly, her fingers at the top button of her dress, slowly undoing it.

"I'm fine," Bianca whispers. "Take your mind off it."

"Hey, I'm *driving*," Beckett says, his head turning lightning-fast between the road and Bianca, now on the second button.

"Don't crash," she purrs, undoing yet another one as we go over a bump, tits bouncing deliciously again.

I'm pretty sure she's not wearing a bra as her fingers undo the last few, the bodice of her dress now totally undone. She bites her lip and rubs her hands over the fabric covering her, shadows all that I can see through the open slit.

"You're the one who lost her," I growl at Beckett, reaching forward and pulling the dress open.

I was right. No bra, just her perfect, luscious breasts with their rosy nipples, stiff against the air, perfectly framed by the bodice. They bounce and sway with the motion of the Jeep, and I'm instantly rock-hard.

I reach out, caress one between my fingers as Bianca leans sideways in her seat, the seatbelt off. The pebbled skin is soft beneath my fingers, and I can already see her wicked smile fading, that look of pure *lust* coming onto her face.

Our dirty girl is insatiable, and I *love* it. I love that she can't get enough of us, that even now she wants us, taking her top off while we're still bouncing down a dirt road through the forest.

"Good thing there's no other people on this road," I say, leaning forward so I can grab her tits with both hands, squeezing and kneading.

Bianca arches her back, her breath quickening. I swear the dress she's wearing was *made* for sex, and there's something so dirty about that that I want to explode.

"Why's that?" she whispers.

I lean further forward, squeezing her perfect breasts hard with my hands, capturing her mouth with mine. She moans, putting her hands on mine and helping me squeeze, pushing her tits against me.

"Because I can't wait to get home to fuck you," I whisper back.

Her lust-filled eyes dart over to Beckett, who's slowed the car, eyes darting back and forth between us and the road, and I laugh as I lower my head to her ear, her neck.

"We can always show him what he's missing and maybe he'll get a turn when we get home," I murmur in her ear. "Think you'd like that, Princess? One of us after the other?"

She bites her red lip between her teeth, and I put one hand on her knee, sliding my hand up her thigh.

"I already have," she reminds me.

Beckett floors it over another bump, and all three of us fly into the air a little, landing with an *oof*.

"It's too dangerous to fuck in the car," Beckett growls, but I just laugh.

"Scoot forward," I tell Bianca, and she does.

In moments I'm in her seat, pulling her onto my lap, her legs wide around mine. I've got a nipple in one hand and in the other I'm pulling her skirt up, seeking her wetness with my fingers.

I find it easily, and Bianca moans, writhing on my lap.

"You didn't wear a bra *or* panties," I murmur in her ear. "Don't you want to show him? Prove that all along you wanted to get fucked before we got back home?"

She's half-coy, half-innocent as she pushes her skirt over her thighs, then her hips. I pull her legs apart, and I know that Beckett can see that she's bare, can *smell* how turned on she is right now, even if he can't quite see her pink lips.

But just in case, I run two fingers between them, opening her for us both. I'm taunting him, and I know it, but he *lost* her.

This is his punishment.

"I'm not surprised," I tell her. "You're so wet you're soaking *my* pants through, and we're not even halfway there."

I knead her breasts. She gasps, moans, and I'm that much harder for knowing she *planned* this.

Bianca reaches back, arching off the seat, and undoes my pants, reaches in. She sits right in front of my cock and leans back, the pressure of our bodies together lighting me on fire.

"You don't seem to mind," she murmurs back.

In the driver's seat, Beckett growls. Bianca reaches

over, strokes one thigh, and he nearly drives off the road. I shove my pants further down, and suddenly we're skin-to-skin and I'm done waiting.

I lift Bianca up. Her hand comes off Beckett's thigh, grabs the car door for support, and I lower her right onto my cock.

"Kieran," she gasps, her head tilting back. Almost automatically, she puts one hand to a breast, pinching her own nipple.

Beckett growls again. Now he's not doing much more than glancing at the road while he stares at Bianca.

"Did you think about my cock every time a breeze went up your skirt?" I ask into her ear. "Every time your skirt swished against your thigh, did you wish it was my hand, reaching for your swollen little pussy?"

"Yes," she moans. "God, I love the way you feel."

Beckett's got an erection the size of Mount Everest. Good. This is what he gets for nearly losing her.

We go over a bump and Bianca bounces on my lap, forcing me even deeper, and she gasps, clutching at the car door.

"Oh, *fuck*," she breathes, the words almost reverent, both hands on her tits now. "Oh God, Kieran, fuck me just like that."

I dig my hands into her hips and grind her down onto me, feeling her pussy stretch and flex, fluttering with every bump we go across as she moans like crazy. Before I know it, she's leaning back onto me, writhing and arching, and I'm fucking her hard while barely moving at all, the dirt road below us doing all the work.

It's fucking *good*. It's new. No one's ever ridden my cock as we drove down a bumpy dirt road before, but it's fucking incredible. The way that I can feel every millimeter of Bianca's pussy as she moans, the way every rut and bump pushes me deeper than before. The way she's practically impaled on my cock, helpless with pleasure.

"I'm gonna come," Bianca whimpers, her pussy clenching around me yet again, the soft sensations making the heat pool in my belly. "Kieran, fuck me until I come."

The car swerves and slows, Beckett glancing over yet again, one hand off the wheel and reaching for Bianca's thigh. She looks at him through heavy-lidded eyes, a moan on her red lips, as he grabs her knee, pulls it toward him, opening her thighs even further.

He crawls his hand up toward her clit, still glancing at the road every so often. I'm half afraid he's going to run us into a tree, but I don't even care at this point. Bianca's head goes back on my shoulder as he starts rubbing her swollen clit, wet with her juices, and she moans at the roof of the Jeep.

"Oh God," she moans. "I love it when you both

fuck me."

I grab her knee, lift her leg over the console so she's straddling me at an angle, her back still against me, but now Beckett has a perfect view of my thick cock inside Bianca while he rubs her clit.

"We're not both fucking you," I tell her. "Not yet."

"I want you to," she breathes.

The thought nearly sends me over the edge: Beckett in one hole, my cock in the other, Bianca between us coming so hard she can barely move.

We go over a hard bump, shoving my cock deep inside Bianca, and she makes a noise that's half-moan, half-scream of pleasure as she's still kneading her own breasts, riding my cock in the car while Beckett massages her clit, one leg slung over the center console.

It's nearly pornographic, except it's only for us. It'll only ever be for us.

"I'm gonna come," she gasps. "Make me come, *please*."

Beckett careens around a curve in the bumpy road. We're nearly there, and just as I realize that Bianca's body shakes, her moans twice as loud.

Her pussy spasms around me, so tight it nearly hurts, her back arching as she cries out wordlessly.

"I knew you fucking liked this," I growl into her ear, so close myself that my cock feels like heated steel. "I knew how bad you needed us to fuck you before you even got home."

Bianca just moans again, her eyelids fluttering, her hips bucking and writhing as she moves on top of me, pussy practically milking my cock.

I last one more second, and then I burst inside her. I grab her by the hips, hold her down so I'm as deep inside her as I can possibly get, and I fill her sweet pussy with stream after stream of come, this glorious terrible road doing all the work.

"I love it when you come inside me," she whispers, her eyelids lowering now, her voice soft and mewling and needy even as she's still pinching and rolling her nipples, hips still moving on top of me.

Beckett takes his hand off her, wrenches the wheel around a turn, and suddenly the cabin is there in front of us. He pulls up in front, brakes hard, and shuts off the car as fast as he possibly can.

Then he leans over, grabs Bianca's head, and kisses her hard while I'm still inside her.

CHAPTER NINETEEN

Beckett

Bianca's lips practically melt under mine as I kiss her hard, her body still writhing with pleasure. I know Kieran's still inside her, but I know she likes this.

She *likes* having both of us in her, one way or another, likes being a plaything for two men at the same time.

And that's good. I could never do this with anyone else, but strangely, I like that I'm kissing her while she's still fucking my best friend. I *like* watching him fuck her while I play with her clit, the way she comes so hard with his cock inside her.

I'm jealous, but I'm something else, too. It wasn't like this with the other girls we've fucked together — that was always about seeing how far we could go, how much the same girl would let us use her at the same time.

But this is different. It could never be like *this* with anyone but her, and I know it.

"Stay there," I growl when I finish the kiss, my hand still grabbing her chin.

Bianca's disheveled, her dress unbuttoned over her tits and hiked up around her waist, but she's still so fucking beautiful it hurts. Maybe *more* beautiful for looking completely wanton like she does, like a woman in need of another good fuck.

I leap out of the car, come around the front, and wrench open Kieran's door before he can. Bianca just smiles at me, still impaled on her cock, as I lift her off of him and stand her in front of me, pushing her back against the seat with him still in it.

"Kieran was right," I say. "Now it's my turn."

She's smiling, biting her lip, but I claim her mouth again, hard and merciless. Watching Kieran fuck her nearly made me crash the car, so out of my mind with lust that I thought we might not make it back here at all.

"I liked it when you watched me," she says, all coyness and innocence at the same time.

I spin her around roughly, bend her over Kieran's lap, his flaccid cock still out.

"Good," I growl, moving one hand up the back of

her thigh, giving her perfect ass a good, hard squeeze. "Because I liked watching you get fucked, Princess, and I'm about to do it again. Only now I'm going to be the one fucking you."

In moments, my pants are undone, my cock out, one hand tangled in her hair. Bianca moans against Kieran's lap as I push the head of my cock to her entrance, already dripping with his juices, but I don't care.

She's not his. She's not mine.

She's *ours*.

I drive my cock into her with a single thrust, as hard and deep as I possibly can. I roar, and she cries out with pleasure, her breath coming fast, her heart pounding so hard I can feel it when I fuck her.

Despite mine being the second cock inside her in as many minutes, she's still so tight it's like she's a glove for my cock, and her whole body jerks and writhes with pleasure as I pull out and fuck her again, even harder the second time.

"Beckett," she whimpers. "Oh God, Beckett."

She's still got her head down on Kieran's lap, and I pull her hair while I fuck her, the black strands wrapped around my fist, so she's standing with her back arched, tits on Kieran's thigh. He reaches down and takes them in his hands, pinching both nipples at once.

Bianca shivers. Her pussy's already fluttering around my thick shaft. I fuck her as deep as I can with every stroke, and each time her body gives me a little jolt of pleasure.

I'm not gonna last long. I can't watch her come, undone and disheveled and the sexiest thing I've ever seen, *then* fuck her and not come like a freight train, but I want her to come again first. She's close, moaning and screaming while I fuck her and Kieran pinches her delicate pink nipples.

He shifts in his seat toward us, and then he's reaching down. He kisses her hard, makes her moans muffled, and then he's got his fingers on her clit while I fuck her, both of us moving furiously at once.

"I need you both," she whispers.

A tremor goes through her body. I pull her hair a little harder.

"I want you both to fuck me," she murmurs. She nearly sounds delirious, but I know she means what she says. "Please, I want you both to—"

I pull out, the ridge of my cock out past her lips, and then I *slam* into her as hard as I fucking can.

"—Fuck me!" she shouts, her voice breaking with pleasure as her words turn into one long moan and she comes, pussy fluttering and writhing and jolting around me. She comes like this is her very first orgasm, moaning into Kieran's mouth, both of us on her at once, sharing in her pleasure.

I completely lose control, fuck her hard and fast and just as she finishes, I'm coming too, unloading my cock into her totally bare, doing my best to fill her up like I know she wants.

Slowly, I let go of her hair, and she crumples forward into Kieran. He wraps his arms around her, even as one of her hands drifts back to me, stroking my hip as she looks over her shoulder with heavy-lidded eyes.

"That satisfy you for another few hours?" I ask, leaning forward and teasing into her ear. "You like knowing that the two of us can barely keep up with you?"

She bites her lip, laughing.

"You're doing just fine," she murmurs back.

• • •

Even though Kieran and I are on edge for the next few days, nothing else happens. We're afraid that poor Günther was set up by the hacker group, that he was some sort of dry run for them.

Maybe they just used him to see how she'd react if she was chased. Maybe they wanted to see if they could get her alone, make her panic.

Or maybe that was a fluke accident and it had

nothing at all to do with them. I've got no idea.

But we don't go out again, not out of sight of the cabin. We cook a lot, we read books. We find a turntable in the mostly-unused study, and the three of us hang out together, trying to appreciate the classical music records we find.

It goes okay. Neither Kieran nor I are particularly into classical music, but at this point, we'll take anything.

A top-secret messenger from the palace shows up one day. He knows the password and the secondary password, has the right seal on his all-wheel-drive, and hands over a message that can be unencrypted using only a book that's already inside the cabin.

The message doesn't tell us much. Only that nothing else has happened and they haven't gotten to the bottom of the conspiracy. The video that broadcast over the airwaves — all digital, obviously — was sent out from some sort of heavily encrypted ISP that originated in North Korea.

To put it lightly, it's unlikely that Voravia will ever convince North Korea to investigate. They don't think the country was involved, but they'll never tell us who *was*.

The message tells us to stay put, at least for a little while longer.

Which is *fine*. Because cabin fever might be setting

in, just a little, but I could spend years in this cabin with Bianca and Kieran and never get bored. She's funny and witty, interested in everything, and Kieran's already my best friend. When there's no fun to be had, the three of us can make it.

Plus, the sex. Bianca's insatiable and she makes me feel that way too, the combination of innocence and pure lust are almost more than I can handle.

She sucks us both off in the shower, swallowing both of us, one after the other, while she rubs herself. We wake up in the middle of the night to her grinding against us in her sleep, so we wake her up and take turns.

To get back at Kieran, one day when he's outside I lock the back door and then we fuck in front of it, Bianca coming hard with two fingers up her ass while he searches frantically for the keys.

She wants *everything*, begs us for it, and it's impossible to say no when she's wet and splayed on the kitchen table with your cock down her throat.

Not that I mind. This is the best thing that's ever happened to me.

• • •

One afternoon, Kieran and I are both reading our books from Belle's in the living room when the door opens and in walks Bianca.

Wearing lingerie.

Yeah, she's got our attention. It's just a sheer white slip, positively *modest* for lingerie, but through it I can see the outline of her stiff nipples as they poke through the fabric, and the cleft of her ass.

She doesn't say anything, but she knows we're watching as she makes her way silently to the kitchen, opens the fridge, and takes out a bottle of champagne. She must have gotten it from the wine cellar without either of us noticing, and then she grabs three champagne glasses and walks for the back door, toward the veranda.

"I'm gonna take a dip in the hot tub," she says, cocking her head slightly to one side, in that way that makes me absolutely *crazy*. "If anyone wants to join?"

CHAPTER TWENTY
Bianca

I slide the glass door shut behind myself carefully, champagne bottle in one hand and glasses in the other, heart beating fast.

Kieran and Beckett *do* something to me. They make me insatiable, make me crave them every second that we're not together. I think they've turned me into a nymphomaniac or something.

It's insane.

And it's not like I didn't think about sex before. I wasn't one of *those* virgins, not like my cousin Aurora, though God knows her husband Declan is banging her six ways from Sunday every night now.

But I had desires. I got myself off. I had sex toys. I even watched porn a couple of times, though I found it kind of hard to get into. The women never look like they're actually enjoying it, you know?

I take the wire cage off the champagne cork, grab it, and pull it out with a loud pop as I glance at the back door. I'm one hundred percent sure that Beckett and Kieran are coming, obviously.

I pour the champagne into my own glass, put the bottle and the other two glasses on the deck floor, turn on the bubbles, and get in, white slip and all.

Instantly, I'm soaked, and the white slip I'm wearing may as well be made of tissue paper. I can see my own nipples clear as day through it, and it's stuck to me like glue, every curve of my entire body vividly outlined.

Strangely, it makes me nervous. Even though I know I shouldn't be, I still am. Nervous that I'm being too aggressive, too forward, and even though I know that I'm obviously wrong, I can't help it.

I swig down the whole glass of champagne, refill my glass, chug that one too. Just as I've refilled my glass again — this time to sip it, thanks — the door opens.

My pulse speeds up, my nipples harden, and my pussy *pounds* with desire. They're not even out here yet, but *this* is what they do to me.

"You wanted company, right?" Beckett's voice says, and he emerges from the door.

Then he stops. He stares, and I bite my lip, relaxing against the side of the hot tub, breasts just barely out of the water, letting him *look*. The way he looks, I can practically *feel* him caressing me, stroking me, squeezing my breasts and biting my nipples just the way I like...

"...Unless you wanted all three glasses of champagne," he says, his voice suddenly less focused.

Behind him Kieran comes out, too, slides the door shut behind him silently.

"I don't mind the company," I say, trying to make my voice sound light. The champagne is taking effect quickly.

Good.

Without another word, both men take off their shirts, then their pants. I watch, practically drooling over their perfectly sculpted bodies, firm abs and bulging biceps. That V that cuts down over their hips, like an arrow pointing at their huge, thick cocks.

Cocks that are both already rock-hard, pointing skyward. I stare. I can't help myself.

"See something you like, Princess?" Beckett growls at me, walking toward the hot tub.

"I see two things," I murmur back, practically licking my lips.

This is what I wanted. Of course it's what I wanted, to fuck them both in the hot tub. But it's not all I want, not tonight.

I lean my head backward, over the lip of the tub, arching my back and letting my breasts come fully out of the water. My nipples pucker instantly with the coolness of wet fabric against them, and I'm breathing harder, already excited.

Beckett steps closer, his powerful frame towering over me, Kieran right next to him. I circle one nipple with a finger, looking up at them, and I lick my lips.

Slowly, Beckett steps forward. He grabs my hair, tugs at it, and I let him pull me down until my head is upside-down, hanging over the lip of the hot tub, his thick cock bobbing in front of my face. His movements are almost dreamy, a little trance-like, even as I move my other hand to my breasts, pinching my nipples between my fingers.

He knows what I want, and he knows it's what he wants. Slowly, he pushes the tip of his cock between my lips, and I open my mouth obligingly, taking in his thick length until he stops against the back of my mouth.

Beckett strokes my throat with his thumb, and at the same time, someone's hand pinches a nipple, making me moan.

"Swallow my cock, Princess," he growls.

I take a deep breath and force my throat to relax. Beckett pushes in, hard, and after a second I feel the head of his cock pop into my throat and he slides the rest of himself in smoothly until my lips are at the bottom of his shaft, my eyes watering.

Above me, he moans, growls, pulls a little harder on my hair, fucking my throat for a few more strokes before pulling back. I gasp for air even as I lick and slurp the juices from his cock and he strokes my neck with his thumb.

"God, I love watching you do that," he murmurs, stepping back.

I swallow, unable to really speak in this position, but I love *doing* it. Even from this position, totally prone and being fucked, I get a sense of power from it, that *I'm* the one making these two powerful, dominant, sexy men lose control.

I love letting them use me however they want. I love that they have total access to my body, anything, anywhere.

Kieran steps forward, and I open my mouth obediently. He doesn't go slow like Beckett does, doesn't pause when he hits my soft palette, just forces me to open my throat and swallow him instantly. I'd moan if I could but he's filling my mouth and throat, hands pinching and rolling at my nipples as I bend backward over the hot tub.

They take turns. By the second time I swallow Kieran, listening to him growling up above me, telling me how pretty I am with my mouth stuffed with cock, I'm already reaching down between my legs, touching myself.

My clit and lips are already swollen with desire, and just touching myself sends a shock of pleasure through my whole body. Kieran pulls out of my throat as I suck him, and Beckett steps forward, his hand tightly around his shaft.

He puts the head of his cock between my lips, and I lick and suck at him, swirling my tongue around, but he doesn't let me take him in any further.

Instead he pulls out again, Kieran taking his place with a groan, my throat bulging. There's a splash as Beckett gets into the hot tub, and I feel myself lifted out of the water, my hand brushed away as Beckett sinks two fingers into my pussy, making my hips buck.

"Seems unfair to make you do it yourself, Princess," he growls, crooking his fingers, making my back arch. "Though I do just fucking *love* how turned on you are after sucking my cock."

The moment Kieran pulls out of my mouth Beckett grabs my hips, flips me over. Now my knees are on the bench of the hot tub, my elbows on the lip, and I'm looking up at Kieran while panting for breath.

My slip is already shoved up over my hips, but Beckett takes a moment to caress my ass as Kieran wipes away the tears from my face with one thumb, his hand moving down, pinching one nipple.

"I'm starting to hope they never find out who made that video," he murmurs. "If never finding out means getting to do this morning and night, I'm happy to live in ignorance forever."

Beckett runs thumb over my pussy, collecting the wetness already gathered there, slides it up and coats my back hole with it. He massages the little pink bud with his thumb carefully, gently, *just* until I moan and then his thick cock is waiting at my entrance, pushing between my lips.

He enters me. I gasp, just like I do every time, because every time I could swear he's gotten bigger, he stretches me further and fills me more. I don't know how I'm always surprised at his length and girth, but I *am*.

With both of them. And I'm surprised at how utterly and completely I want to give myself over to them every time. Just lay down moaning in front of them and tell them to tear their pleasure out of me.

He fucks me hard and fast and I moan, whimper, say his name as my eyes roll. His thumb is still on my back hole, and I push my hips backward with every thrust, *wanting* him to penetrate me there, too.

And then Kieran's got my hair in his hand, guiding his cock to my mouth and I suck him in, swallowing eagerly as he presses the short, curly hairs of his hips against my lips, my nose against his flesh.

"I love when you beg to be fucked from both ends," he growls, thrusting shallowly into my throat, groaning with pleasure.

They fuck me together, in perfect time, thrusting as one. Kieran pulls out sometimes, lets me breathe, but even as I'm gasping for air I'm hungrily licking and sucking his cock, wanting him back inside me even as I buck back against Beckett, wanting him inside *both* holes.

Then, finally: I feel him enter me, fucking me hard with his cock but gently with a finger, just barely sliding inside. Kieran pulls out of my mouth and I moan, pushing back.

"More," I whimper. "Please, God, Beckett, I need *more*."

He pushes another finger into my ass and I throw my head back, groaning. I love how full I feel, and sucking Kieran's cock into my mouth again only adds to the feeling.

He adds a third finger, and my eyes go wide. My knees tremble, and I can't do anything with my mouth at the base of Kieran's cock, but my whole *body* reacts like a series of tiny explosions going off. He fucks me again, this time with his cock *and* his fingers.

I come, moaning and shouting as Kieran pulls out, my hands scrabbling at the edge of the hot tub.

"Oh my God," I whimper, waves of electricity rushing through my whole body as he keeps going, not giving an inch. "Oh God, Beckett, Kieran."

Beckett grabs my hair, pulls my head up, burying himself as deep and hard as he can while I quaver around him.

"Kieran," he growls.

Kieran steps away, leaving the two of us standing there in the hot tub, Beckett stuffing both my holes. I'm still coming, wave after wave hitting me as I'm helpless, pinioned to him.

Kieran crouches down, pulls something from a pants pocket. Tosses it to Beckett.

Beckett pulls his finger from my ass, and even as I whimper in disappointment, I can feel something cool and viscous being poured over my tight back hole. I squirm again, but then Kieran's back, guiding his cock to my mouth and I take him in, licking and sucking at the head, sliding my lips down the shaft as far as I can reach.

Beckett grabs my hip and pulls his still rock-hard cock from my pussy. I whimper, my lips around Kieran's cock.

"No," I manage to say. "Come inside me."

Beckett doesn't say anything, just chuckles.

Then I feel something new. The tip of his cock at my back hole, sliding around in something slippery, one of his hands on my shoulder.

"Relax, Princess," he murmurs, and then he pushes into me.

I gasp, my whole body going rigid, my eyes slamming shut. A hand strokes my hair, gently, and before I know it Kieran's letting me nestle my face against his strong hip, his hands soothing as Beckett takes my hips, pulls me back.

"Oh God," I whisper. I feel like Beckett's cock is splitting me in two, his head impossibly wide and thick, stretching me past my limits.

Beckett just grunts.

"It can't," I whisper, Kieran's hand on my hair. "God, Kieran, it can't..."

"Almost there," Beckett growls, his hands tracing patterns on my back. "Just relax like a good girl, and — oh, *fuck*."

There's a moment where I really think I *can't*, I think Beckett is going to tear me in half, but then there's an odd popping sensation and it doesn't hurt any more, and I take a quick, short breath in surprise.

And I realize: Beckett's in my ass.

"I told you," he says, his breathing heavy, labored. "Jesus, Bianca, you feel so fucking good..."

He slides in, slowly. Gently. He goes millimeter by millimeter as I moan, gasp, sometimes licking Kieran's cock. Little by little he buries himself hilt-deep inside me until suddenly, he's all the way in.

It's strange, but it's wonderful. It's like electrical charges zipping across my skin, feels good in ways I could never have imagined.

He starts fucking my ass, the tight bud still stretched around him, and he's careful and gentle but I can tell he wants *more*. He wants to fuck my ass hard and fast, and I want to give him *everything*.

Then Kieran's cock is in front of my mouth, and I take him in again, but now he's merciless, pushing it into my throat, making me swallow him again.

Heat blossoms inside me. God, this is so dirty, so wrong, so *filthy*. I'm a princess, I shouldn't be deep-throating one man while another one fucks my ass.

But it feels so *good*. It feels so good and so *wrong* that I'm moaning every time Kieran lets me breathe, I'm thrusting back against Beckett, letting him bury his cock inside my back hole as deeply as he possibly can.

And I'm about to come again. I'm going to come like this, a cock in my ass and a cock in my throat, and I'm going to come harder than I ever have before.

They both fuck me a little harder, and I moan a little louder, their hands everywhere as they growl dirty things at me, but it only makes the heat blossom inside me faster, brings me closer to the brink.

"Come," Beckett finally says. "I want to feel you come with my cock in your ass, you sweet filthy thing."

He thrusts into me harder than ever before, my eyes rolling back in my head with pleasure.

"Come for us," he says again, and this time I *do*.

It's a bomb going off, it's a chandelier shattering, it's a tsunami breaking over my head and threatening to drown me. I've never come like this before, from these sensations, and I'm completely unprepared for what it's going to feel like or how *good* it does.

I shake, I shiver. My whole body jolts and then before I know it, Kieran is grabbing my hair, pushing my lips all the way down his cock, Beckett thrusting all the way into me at the exact same time and they *explode* in unison, one of them filling my mouth and the other filling my ass with jolt after jolt of their sticky liquid.

I love it. I love when they drag orgasms out of me like this. I love feeling them come inside me, knowing that *I* made them do this. I love swallowing them and feeling them drip down my thigh later, a reminder of what I've been up to.

It's dirty and messy and probably *wrong* but it's ours, and I wouldn't give it up for anything.

Kieran pulls out of my mouth, already going soft. I swallow one last time and he kisses me, and it's sweet and tender, me on my knees in the hot tub and him standing outside it.

Beckett slides out of my ass, grabbing a nearby towel, and cleans us both off delicately while I kiss Kieran long and hard. Then he wraps his arms around me, turns my head, claims by mouth as his own.

"How do you like belonging to us?" he asks.

"I love it," I whisper back.

CHAPTER TWENTY-ONE

Kieran

The rest of that day feels strange and dreamy, like something's shifted in our relationship. Like something that started based on sheer desire, sheer *lust* has somehow changed.

Bianca's given herself to us completely. Not just her body but her *heart*, and suddenly, I feel even more tender toward her, like she's not only something I need to protect but someone I need to *care* for.

I think I knew it all along. I didn't just hand her my heart. She's had it all this time.

I just hadn't realized it yet.

The night passes, Bianca snuggled in between us. In the morning I wake up hard, my cock already between her legs, and she reaches back and slides me inside her before I'm even properly awake. Beckett's eyes open, and then his hand is on her clit, rubbing and massaging.

Bianca comes first. Then she pulls me out, moves her hips, positions me at her back entrance.

"Please," she says, her beautiful eyes wide, and I do.

I go slow and I'm gentle but she's so fucking tight that I nearly come right there. Just knowing that I'm here, with her, that *this* girl is letting me fuck her like *this*.

I come so hard my ears pop.

• • •

Hours later, there's a knock on the door. Beckett and I both leap to our feet, instantly going for the guns we have stashed in a few drawers around the place. Neither of us like them, but we've been here nearly two weeks and this is the first time someone's knocked.

"Go around that corner," I tell Bianca. "Stay close, but out of sight of the door. Beckett, keep an eye on her, just in case this is a trap again."

They both obey. Good. We can't have a repeat of the Günther situation.

Slowly, my gun hand behind my back, I open the door. Somewhere in my brain I know that a person who wants the three of us dead is unlikely to knock, but you can never be too cautious.

But when I see the person who knocked, I have to rethink that. Just a little.

It's a kid with bad skin and a worse haircut. He's skinny and lanky and can't be more than seventeen, looks totally and completely freaked out at my eye, staring at him from the doorway.

He swallows, and his too-large Adam's apple bobs in his throat.

"Delivery?" he squeaks out, holding up two shopping bags.

And I'm suspicious again. We haven't ordered anything. That's not something we'd do, give that we're hiding out. People in lockdown don't *order groceries*.

"They're not ours," I growl.

He checks a piece of paper.

"Um, is this the ancestral hunting cabin of the family Munchveld?" he asks.

I don't answer.

"Because that's where I'm supposed to deliver it, but if this is the wrong ancestral cabin let me know, my GPS doesn't really work up here and it likes addresses rather than vague descriptions anyway?"

"What is it?"

"What's what?"

I roll my eyes.

"In the bags."

"Um. I don't know, this one's got, like, some bread, and some cheese, and there's a thing of jam and butter, and then on the bottom it looks like, ooh, strawberries, don't know who put things on top of those, not protocol at all, and then there's a whole bunch of apples and like some sort of, I don't know, turnip?"

I frown, watching him root around in the bag. It's

pretty clearly not a bomb from the way he's shoving items left and right, probably squashing the hell out of everything.

"Where's it from?"

"Andersen's, down in Inversberg? My boss said that you meant to order this stuff a couple days ago, but then you left without paying and something got confused in the system but then yesterday it spat out an error saying that your order was still missing, and so we found your account and just charged it to that, it shouldn't be too much, and we figured that it was better to err on the side of..."

"I'll take them, it's fine," I say, opening the door and grabbing the bags. "Thanks. Sorry for the mix-up."

"Oh! No problem, I've always wanted to see the Munchveld ancestral cabin in person, my grandma was always going on about it..."

I give the poor kid a hard look. He jams his hands into his pockets.

"Right! Have a nice day, sir," he says, and turns around, walking back to the SUV he came in and I close the door, locking all three locks.

"We got groceries?" Beckett says.

"Yup," I say.

I'm still slightly nervous that this was some sort of recon for the hacker group, that something just happened that I don't understand, but there are no alarms going off. Nothing about this scenario really made me suspicious, once it got explained — my family *has* had this cabin for a long time.

We *do* order groceries from Andersen.

That really *was* a pimple-faced delivery boy.

I explain the whole situation with the mix-up to Beckett and Bianca, and we stash the groceries in the fridge. It'll be nice to have fresh stuff tonight, after all, and then we forget the whole thing. Write it off as a weird quirk that happens in small towns, where everyone knows everything.

A few hours later I'm doing a crossword in the living room when Bianca walks past me, tossing an apple up and down in one hand.

"I'm gonna go have a snack and read in the study," she says. "My night to make dinner?"

"Sounds good," I say, and she walks off.

CHAPTER TWENTY-TWO

Beckett

The sun's going down as I wander into the kitchen, looking for a snack. I open the fridge, rooting around in there for a bit: some salami, a few tubs of yogurt, about twenty apples.

I guess Bianca wasn't kidding when she said she really liked apples.

"Have you seen Bianca?" Kieran asks, wandering in as well. He looks over my shoulder into the fridge while the two of us both try to find a snack.

"Not a for a while," I say. "I think she was gonna go read."

"Hmm," Kieran says, but something in his voice worries me, and suddenly I'm trying to remember the last time I *did* see Bianca.

Is she in trouble? Something dangerous?

Normally I wouldn't be concerned about an adult woman being alone for a few hours, but these aren't exactly normal circumstances.

I shut the fridge, and I'm met with Kieran's frown.

"I'll go see what she's up to," I say, forcing my voice to stay calm. "She said she'd make dinner tonight, right?"

"Right," Kieran echoes, the scowl even in his voice.

It's fine, I tell myself as I walk out of the kitchen and into the hallway, past the living room.

She just got lost in a book. It happens.

She's not in her bedroom or either of ours. The bathrooms are all empty, and when I peek outside, she's not there either.

The door to the study is nearly shut, the lights inside on. My heart is thudding at my ribcage as I push it open, praying that she's inside because if she's not here, she's *gone.*

But there she is, curled up sideways in her favorite reading chair. The book has crumpled a little in her lap, closing on itself. She's probably lost her place.

"Hey, Bianca," I say gently.

She doesn't wake up. I guess she's tired, so I shrug, starting to close the door.

"Wait," Kieran says, his voice low and dark.

Adrenaline sizzles through my veins again, and I

glance at him, then at her.

And I start to realize: something's wrong. I don't know what, but the longer I look at Bianca, the more the feeling grows that she's not just asleep, she's *out*.

"Bianca," Kieran growls, his voice low and gravelly.

He strides across the room, his foot accidentally kicking a half-eaten apple.

"Bianca. Wake up," he gruffs, grabbing her by the shoulder and shaking her.

The books falls from her lap and her head lolls at a strange angle. In half a second I'm there, fingers pressed to her neck as I feel for a pulse, Kieran's face next to her mouth.

I'm terrified. I feel like I'm falling down a bottomless pit, my body wheeling freely, more afraid than I've ever been in my life as I wait the milliseconds for a heartbeat, praying to any god who'll listen that she has one.

It feels like I wait a hundred long years, the world fizzling in front of my eyes, spinning out of control.

No. No, not her. Take me instead, take both of us.

Just not Bianca.

And then, at last, there it is: one thump of her jugular vein, slow and sluggish but *there*.

She's alive.

"Breathing," Kieran growls.

"We've gotta get her to town," I say, standing. I'm

still nauseous, still feel like I'm falling down that endless pit, but she's alive. That's step one, at least, the first of a hundred steps to get her help, get her out of here because we've failed her, somehow, Kieran and I tried, and we fucked this up—

"Come on," Kieran barks, and I slide my arms underneath Bianca's limp form, lifting her body in my hands.

"Grab that apple," I say as I carry her out, the words an afterthought. But somewhere deep down, I know that that's the only thing in here that doesn't fit, the only odd piece to this puzzle.

We head to the Jeep without talking. We're not even wearing shoes or coats, just t-shirts and sweatpants, but neither of us gives a shit. I get into the back seat with Bianca, resting her head on my lap, stroking her hair. Kieran gets into the driver's seat and half a second later we're tearing down the bumpy dirt road in the dark.

I hold her close, absolutely fucking terrified. I don't know what happened and I don't know how to fix it.

"I'm sorry," I whisper. "I'm sorry we fucked up, I'm sorry we didn't protect you, I'm sorry..."

I squeeze her closer, even as we fly over a huge rut, Kieran's hands white-knuckled on the steering wheel.

"I'm sorry for everything," I whisper. "I love you, Bianca."

Kieran's eyes flash in the rearview mirror, full of

pain and regret and torment.

"*We* love you," I correct myself.

• • •

There's no hospital in Inversberg. It's far too small, so we just drive onto the cobblestone street in front of the first open store we find, and Kieran sprints inside without bothering to turn off the car while I just sit in the back seat, holding Bianca.

I feel powerless, more powerless than I ever have before. I don't even know what's wrong with her, what's happened, or how to fix it.

I just keep telling her unconscious form, over and over again, that we love her.

Moments later, Kieran sprints back out.

"The shop owner's called the town doctor," he says, his voice tight and panicked as he smooths one hand over Bianca's hair.

I notice he's shaking. I notice *I'm* shaking, and for a split second we lock eyes, both acknowledging the shared emotion between us.

"He's also calling the hospital so they can send an ambulance, but... it could be a while," he says, his voice nearly breaking.

"It's already been a while," I whisper.

Kieran doesn't answer. We both just sit there, both

silently praying on our own.

Soon, the doctor comes, and then everything is pandemonium. He has us bring her out of the car, lay her down on the cobblestones, head back. He quizzes us endlessly about what she's done that day, what she ate, what she did, what book she was reading, but he doesn't have answers either.

A small crowd gathers. Bianca's still breathing, her heart still beating, but nothing has changed. She's not waking up. She only seems half-alive, her heart beating glacially slow, like she's been put in suspended animation.

Suddenly, there's a whirring noise above us, a breeze stirring our hair, and I look up to see a helicopter. I don't even process it at first, not until it disappears behind a building and the town doctor stands, snapping his bag shut.

"Come on!" he shouts.

I pick her up again. Follow him, feeling empty and hollow, to a clearing a few blocks away where there's a stretcher waiting outside a medical helicopter.

Reality suddenly snaps back as the paramedics run toward us, full tilt, and suddenly I'm *alive* again. I put her on the stretcher, help buckle her in, stroke her hair, help push her back because this I've done before. Never with the girl I love, but I've been in this scenario.

Behind me, Kieran is giving someone the rundown

of everything that happened today in short, clipped sentences as the woman nods, taking notes on a pad.

Finally, she's strapped into the helicopter, and the blades start turning again. The paramedics duck their heads and run back, but at the last second, Kieran runs after them.

"WAIT!" he screams, waving his arms.

From the helicopter, one turns.

"SHE ATE THIS!" he shouts at the top of his lungs, handing over Bianca's half-eaten apple. It's a wreck by now, but the paramedic nods, taking it in one gloved hand.

Kieran steps back. The helicopter doors shut.

It lifts away, Bianca inside. I know she's in better hands than ours now. I know that if she's going to have a chance, it's with them, at a hospital, not with us.

But I can't help but feel as though something's breaking inside me, splintering apart as I watch her leave without knowing if we'll ever see her again.

The helicopter disappears over the trees. Kieran turns to me, face ashen and grim.

"Come on," he says. "We're going to the hospital."

CHAPTER TWENTY-THREE

Bianca

I'm in a maze. It's a hedge maze, the walls towering above me, and I'm walking slowly. The sun is shining above but the hedges are too tall, the sun at too much of an angle for the light to hit me, so I'm covered in deep shadows, feet moving even though I can barely feel them.

This seems familiar, I think. *I've been here before. I've done this before.*

I round a corner, round another corner. I find a dead end, and there's a stone bench with a garden gnome sitting under it.

So familiar.

I turn, leave the dead end, and then it hits me: this is the hedge maze at Castle Verginogne, where my parents took me when I was six. We were standing at the entrance, reciting formalities with a diplomat, when for some reason, I broke free from my parents' hands and ran full-tilt into the maze.

They followed, but I was already gone around three turns.

I was lost for *hours*.

I keep wandering. My feet don't hurt, I'm not hungry, I don't have to pee, I just... wander. Every so often I'd swear I can hear someone calling my name and I stand still, listening with my whole body, but I'm pretty sure it's just my imagination.

There's no one calling my name. There's no one here at all except me, and I just keep walking, running into dead ends, turning around, taking another path.

Sometimes the dirt under my feet feels strange, like it's sticking to me. Sometimes the leaves on the hedges feel *wrong*, a little too thin, like if I concentrated hard enough they might not really be real, but then everything corrects and I lose that feeling.

And I walk on, and on.

• • •

I walk for a long, long time. It might be days. It might be *weeks*, I just know that I don't really mind. Nothing ever hurts, I never get tired.

The longer I walk, the more this doesn't feel like reality. Sometimes I'll see something — a bench, a gnome, a work shovel left out — look away, turn back, and it'll be different. Sometimes it'll feel like my feet are being sucked half an inch into the dirt or like my hand is going through the hedge.

Sometimes the maze switches on me. I'll walk past a turn, look back, and it'll be gone.

It happens more and more, but I keep walking. Just walk. *Just walk.*

I round a corner, and strangely, there's a refrigerator. I frown. There's never been a fridge here before, and I go to it, open it.

Inside there's a single apple. I'm not hungry, but I take it even though it feels strange in my hand. Oddly heavy, too cold, like its surface is covered in velvet but it's not. It's just an apple.

I turn away from the fridge and as I do, I forget all about the apple.

The hedge maze is gone. Well, sort of. Almost. Where there used to be a maze now there's a wide-open space, still hemmed in by the hedges around the border, taller than ever, nothing but dirt and grass and hedge for as far as I can see.

There's no exit. There's no entrance. It's like I've always been in this maze, and even though I *know* that's not true, I can't think of a time before. I can't imagine a time after.

I just squint against the sudden sun, holding one hand up over my eyes. I swear it's getting slowly brighter, bearing down, so bright I can barely open my eyes.

And I've got that sensation again that someone is calling my name, even though I can't hear it, I just *know* it.

Bianca. Bianca. *Bianca*...

CHAPTER TWENTY-FOUR

Kieran

Beckett and are sitting in the hospital waiting room. It's been two days since the helicopter brought Bianca here, two days of Europe's best doctors running every test they could find, the top scientists scratching their heads over the half-eaten apple.

We've heard a thousand things, and so have her parents, here from Voravia. They think it was something in the apple. It wasn't the apple. She breathed in a poison, she had a minor heart attack, she had a stroke, there's a brain tumor so small they can't see it, she has some kind of glandular imbalance.

In short, no one has any fucking clue what's happened to Bianca or why she's been unconscious for nearly three days. All they have is theories and hypotheses, and most of the time, they won't let us in to see her.

It's around two in the afternoon when the main nurse sticks her head in. Her parents look up at the same time we do, and the nurse comes, sits primly on a chair in front of us.

"They think they've found the poison," she says with no introduction.

Beckett and I both sit up straighter. Her mother clutches her father's arm, both of them still silent.

"It's very rare, and frankly, it's very *strange*, which is why no one thought to test for it sooner," she says. "There are simply thousands and thousands of poisons, and so testing always takes time, meaning that—"

"What was it?" her mother says, her face white.

"Right. Yes, of course," the nurse goes on, looking down. "A neurotoxin from the Amazonian Bread Beetle. Normally, it kills someone by causing their lungs to slowly stop working so they simply can't breathe."

I crack a knuckle, holding my own breath.

"But," the nurse goes on. "In exactly the right dose, it can dramatically slow breathing and heartrate, giving the victim a near-dead appearance that can last for hours, days, weeks, or..."

She shrugs.

"No one is really sure, because it's incredibly hard to get, so there simply isn't much information."

"Will she wake up?" her father rumbles, his wife still squeezing his arm.

The nurse smiles.

"Luckily, the antidote is simple, and we've already given it to her. She should be awake within the hour. She's already stirring."

. . .

We wait outside Bianca's door, anxious. Her parents are inside, her mother crying, and I can just barely hear Bianca's voice over the noise.

Finally, her father comes to the door, calls us in. Bianca's propped up on pillows, tubes sticking out from both her arms, but she smiles at us despite the huge circles under both eyes.

"Good morning, beautiful," Beckett says, taking one hand.

I take the other and simply kiss the back.

"Hi," Bianca whispers.

Behind us, her parents step quietly from the room.

. . .

After that, everything happens quickly. Bianca still

has to undergo a thousand more tests, scans, MRIs, the whole deal, but it's all downhill. There's no lasting brain damage, and it's decided that the safest place for her is my family's stronghold.

I have workers rip out anything that connects to the internet, then configure all the power to be run from a generator. I don't want *anything* in her wing to be connected to the grid. I'm not taking chances again, because it's our fault that this happened to her.

We should have never taken her into Inversberg. We should never have let our guard down like that, should never have been so careless.

Bianca's moved in absolutely secrecy, at three o'clock in the morning. She's fine, though still a little weak, the effects of the poison finally draining from her system.

She's got her own suite in the castle, her own everything, and Beckett and I can stay right next door. I haven't talked to her parents at all, but I get the distinct sense that they know *something* is going on, but they haven't said anything, and neither have I.

For days, the two of us wait on her hand and foot, even when she tells us not to. We insist on bringing her anything she needs ourselves, plumping her pillows, getting her more tea, rearranging her footrest. But she gets stronger day by day, and before long, that *wicked* look is back in her eyes.

The look that says, *I remember the hot tub.*

I force myself to ignore it. She needs to really be better, be fully recovered before we can do *that* again, no matter how badly I ache for her.

So I settle for jerking off twice a day in the shower, imagining fucking Bianca deep, her pussy clenching around me as Beckett slides his cock down her throat.

I imagine the way she moans, the way her body moves like she's hungry for me.

I imagine pushing my cock into the tight bud of her back hole, how she'd gasp and pant for breath. I think of the way she'd *scream* when she came that way.

And of course, of *course*, I think of Beckett joining me. I think of us taking her together, the way she begged us to. I think of Bianca flooded with so much pleasure that she can't talk, can barely move.

And then I come into the shower drain, and I do it again a few hours later, because all the jerking off in the world isn't a substitute for *her.*

CHAPTER TWENTY-FIVE
Beckett

A week goes by, then two. Bianca recovers in Kieran's castle, and though being near her without *doing* anything taps every last strength reserve I've got, the doctors said she needed to take it easy.

And even though she looks at us as wickedly as ever, even though I know she still *wants* us, I resist. It's not worth hurting her over.

One day we're all at dinner when one of Kieran's palace guards comes up to him and asks him *sotto voce* if the castle has a top-secret secure location.

Kieran just looks at the man like he's insane.

"It's a fortress," he says. "Of course it does."

We don't even eat dessert, just go down to the basement, then the sub-basement. Kieran turns a lion sculpture the right way and reveals a hidden room, talks very seriously with his security men. Inside is a beautiful, oval wood table with high-backed chairs all around it, and we sit.

I'm watching Bianca nervously the whole time, wondering if she's under attack. Wondering if we're all going to be under attack, if there's some kind of robot swarm heading our way.

Minutes after we sit, a straight-backed, suited man comes in and stands at the head of the table.

"I'm General Tsukor of the Voravian military," he begins.

My back is ramrod straight.

"And I'm here to update you on the threat to the princess's life."

He opens a manila folder, taking out a small stack of handouts. I wonder why he's not using the projector at the front of the room, but then I realize that anything with a wireless signal — anything that connects to the outside world — is a threat.

"On the first page you'll see a schematic of how the initial broadcast threatening the princess went out. The second page involves the Inversberg grocers, the third the mechanics of the incredibly poisonous Amazonian Bread Beetle, and the fifth is what we can tell you about the ongoing plan to capture the remaining at-large members of this terrorist hacker cell," he says.

No one seems to have any questions, so the General dives right in.

The explanations are long, technical, and they lose me a couple of times. All right, they lose me more than a couple of times, when I can't tell if what he's saying are acronyms or words, but the jist of it is this:

Hacking into the television signal wasn't that hard, especially since it's all done via digital internet signals anyway, the heyday of *actual* airwaves being long past. They cloaked themselves more than well enough, and were impossible to find.

They found Bianca again because she came into town. It seems this group hacked into millions of cameras — closed circuit cameras, stoplight cameras, security cameras, you name it — and had facial recognition software running, making it easy enough to find her if she so much as went somewhere with security.

Shit, I think, staring at the handout. *I had no idea that was possible.*

I don't feel inadequate often, but I do right now.

Once they knew where she was and who she was with, it was a matter of guessing that we were at the hunting cabin, getting into Andersen's ordering system, and making a fake order to be delivered to us. Why they chose the Bread Beetle is beyond anyone's guess, though.

The delivery boy had nothing to do with it. The grocery store had nothing to do with it. They were just pawns in this stupid, fucked up game that I still don't understand.

Voravian intelligence, working with Interpol, has caught most of the ringleaders and they're on the trail of the others, though of course they don't say too much about it.

"And that's about it," the General says, snapping his folder closed. "Any questions?"

"Why Bianca?" Kieran asks, his voice loud in the small room.

The General rubs his hands together, and he looks like he's about to say something, then stops himself.

"We're not sure," he finally tells us.

Kieran's eyes narrow, his mouth making a hard line.

"You were about to say something."

"I'd rather not."

"You have an idea, though."

"It's unconfirmed, I'm afraid."

"But there's something."

The General looks down at his papers, running his fingers over the folder before looking up at us.

"Tell us," Kieran demands. "Tell *her*."

He doesn't want to. That much is clear, but he stands a little straighter.

"It will come off as quite childish, but I assure you, it's the best motive we could find. We're still searching for another, but so far, nothing has surfaced."

"What is it?" Bianca asks, speaking up for the first time.

He swallows.

"Jealousy, Your Highness," he says.

We all frown simultaneously.

"Of me?" Bianca says, sounding baffled.

"In our investigation we found an enlightening discussion that took place on a private, encrypted message board," he goes on, obviously uncomfortable. "It seems that one of the masterminds had commented on Princess Bianca's physical charms in front of his girlfriend, and she was quite upset by this. He was already part of a radical anti-monarchy group, of course, but it seems that one thing led to another, and to prove to his girlfriend that he thought quite highly of her, he... orchestrated *this*."

The room goes completely, *totally* silent. You could hear an ant fart, it's so quiet.

"You're kidding," Bianca finally says.

He clears his throat.

"I'm afraid not," he says. "And we're quite certain there are other factors at play, of course, but so far, this is the best lead we've got."

Silence again.

184

"I ought to be going if there are no further questions," the General says. "I'm glad you're doing well and best wishes, Your Highness, Lords."

We all murmur goodbyes, but then lapse into silence again after he leaves.

It takes a while, but Bianca finally speaks up.

"That's just *silly*," she says, staring at the table. "Who would...? I mean, just...?"

I stand, holding out a hand to her.

"Come on," I say gently. "Let's go to bed, maybe it'll make sense in the morning."

We leave the super-secret sub-basement and ascend back to the upper floor of the palace. Bianca doesn't let go of my hand the whole time, Kieran close behind us.

We haven't bothered keeping our relationship a secret. Not that we've exactly broadcast it to the world, either, but it's no secret. The guards know, the people at the palace know, half of Griskold knows. And it doesn't matter.

No. *She's* what matters.

At the door to her suite, Bianca turns to us, lips red as ever, skin pale, hair dark, eyes blue. She bites her lip, looking from me to Kieran and back.

"Come read me a bedtime story?" she asks, her smile and voice bordering on wicked.

Kieran sucks in a breath, and I swallow hard.

"What kind of story?" I ask.

"One about two princes and one princess," she says, looking up at me, her voice dropping to a purr. "I want to hear *all* about their happy ending."

CHAPTER TWENTY-SIX

Bianca

The words are barely out of my mouth when Beckett scoops me up and carries me to the bed. It's been nearly two weeks since we've done *anything*, because I've been recuperating, but all three of us know that today the doctors cleared me again for *strenuous activities*.

And I know exactly what *strenuous activity* I'd like to participate in.

Beckett tosses me onto the bed, so hard I bounce, breathless, my skirt already coming up. Both of them follow me onto the huge, plush surface, and before I can even come up on my elbows they're on either side of me.

Beckett grabs my face, kissing me roughly. His tongue plunders my mouth, and he lets out a long, low groan as he does, his cock against my hip already rock-hard, straining against his zipper.

"I don't think I can go slow tonight," he growls, thumb tracing my lip.

"Then don't," I say, my voice half-whisper, half-moan as I suck his thumb into my mouth.

On my other side Kieran pushes his hand up my thigh, pushing my skirt over my hips. In one motion he takes my panties in his fist, tugging them tight against me, and turns my face toward him, Beckett's thumb trailing from my mouth.

My body's already rigid with desire, my thighs clamped around Kieran's fist, his knuckles against my clit and pussy. I grind against him, mouth open, moaning.

"You've fantasized long and hard about what we're going to do tonight, haven't you?" he says, his voice low and rough.

He tightens his fist on my panties, pushing his knuckles against my bare heat. They're already slippery with my juices, my breathing coming faster and faster.

"What are you going to do?" I ask, even though I think I know.

Kieran kisses me hard, pressing his mouth against mine. I'm helpless against my desire for him, for *them*, and I can only whimper as Beckett practically rips my blouse off and shoves my bra out of the way, both of my breasts in his hands.

God, it feels so good to be shared.

"We're going to fuck you together like you've been begging us to do," Kieran whispers, his hand unfurling from my panties.

His fingers slide around my clit, and my hips buck, rolling against him as his words rock through me.

Both of them. Together. God, I've barely thought about anything else for two weeks. Just seeing them around the palace makes me impossibly wet, so aroused that I'm forever slipping into bathrooms just so I can get myself off for some release.

"He's going to fuck your sweet, wet little pussy," Kieran murmurs.

He slides three fingers into my slippery, needy entrance, and I move my hips up to meet him, a little moan escaping me.

"And I'm finally going to claim your ass," he finishes.

Deftly, he moves one finger from my pussy downward, circling it slickly around my puckered back hole, sending a shiver through my whole body.

I think of Beckett, bending me over in the hot tub, stretching and spreading me.

I remember how hard I came, how it felt totally unlike anything else I'd ever done.

"Yes," I whisper, just as Beckett bites a nipple,

making my back arch. "Yes!"

Beckett just chuckles and hooks his thumbs under my skirt. In seconds I'm unzipped, my skirt and panties on the floor as he rolls me toward him.

I hear Kieran getting undressed, and then he's pressed against me, his thick cock against my lower back.

I don't wait. I *can't* wait any longer. Beckett kisses me hard and deep, still caressing my nipples, as I sling one knee over him, reaching back for Kieran's cock. It's hard as steel in my hand, somehow even bigger than I remember, and I arch, guiding him to my entrance.

He fucks me deep with one hard stroke, driving himself balls-deep just as Beckett kisses me again. I nearly shout into his mouth as every nerve ending in my body lights up, like I've just been plugged in for the first time.

Beckett just laughs, trailing his hand down my torso until it's between my legs. He starts rubbing my clit and Kieran starts fucking me, slow and deep, my hand clawing at his thigh.

"You know what my two favorite things are?" he asks.

I can't even answer. I can barely look at him, my eyes constantly threatening to roll backward into my head with the perfect, pure sensations.

"My second favorite is watching Kieran fuck you," he says, his fingers tightening on my clit.

Kieran drives himself home again with a long, low groan.

"Oh *God*," I whimper, eyelids fluttering. Beckett's fingers move faster, bringing me toward the edge.

"I couldn't stand for anyone else to do it," he goes on. "But getting to *watch* you turn from a sweet, demure, perfect princess into a dirty girl, stuffed with cock and begging for more? Fucking delectable, Bianca."

I'm about to come, between Beckett's fingers and Kieran's cock. I've held out for as long as I can, but between the two of them, I'm nearly powerless.

"My *very* favorite is fucking you myself, though," he goes on. "I love fucking your pussy, your mouth, your ass. There's nothing like being inside you, Princess."

Beckett pinches my clit gently between two fingers just as Kieran thrusts into me as hard as he can, his cock hitting *that* spot so perfectly, and with that, I fall over the edge, grabbing at Beckett's shirt, clawing at Kieran's thigh, whimpering and moaning and maybe even shouting.

I feel like I'm a mountain that's just become a volcano, the heat splitting me apart so that my top flies off, lava running down my sides in rivulets, but they don't stop. Beckett's fingers keep moving on my clit, jolting my whole body at once, and Kieran pulls out, hit cock slippery and dripping.

Behind me, he rolls over. A drawer opens, closes, there's the sound of a bottle being snapped open, and I reach behind myself, grab Kieran's head just as his slick fingers find my back hole.

One slips in and I bite my lip, close my eyes, arch back. He slips in another, and another, and now I'm desperate, pushing back against him, wanting *more*.

"That's right," he growls into my ear. "Fuck my hand, Princess. Show me what you want."

I do, as hard as I can, but it's not enough and Kieran *knows* it. After a moment he chuckles, pulling his fingers out, biting my ear.

I don't even hesitate. I *can't*. I lock eyes with Beckett as I grab Kieran's cock, slippery with a combination of lube and my own pussy juices, and guide it to my back hole.

"I love it when you're dirty for us," he whispers into my ear.

Then he grabs my hip, holding me still, and slowly pushes himself into me. Beckett's fingers are still dancing on my clit, rubbing me furiously, and as Kieran's cock slowly stretches my back hole, opening me up, Beckett kisses me hard.

He eases in, slowly but firmly, and I close my eyes, biting my lip. It feels so *strange*, right on the edge of pain, and I can't help but think *this will never work, he's too big, he's way too big to fit there* —

But then, just as I'm about to whimper and move away and tell him I can't *possibly* the head of his cock pops through my tight ring of muscle and it doesn't hurt any more.

He pauses. I breathe, and Kieran strokes my body in long strokes, from hip to torso, squeezing my nipples. He doesn't move, and I can feel myself flex and clench, my body wanting *more* of him.

"Such a good girl," he murmurs into my ear. "Fitting my cock into your ass on the first try. You like the way it feels when I stretch you out?"

I arch my back, flexing backward, my hand on his hip again. A little more of Kieran slides into me and I swear sparks explode all around my vision.

"More," I gasp, my knee still slung over Beckett's hips, sandwiched between my two lovers. "God, more, *please*."

He gives it to me. He goes slow, fucking my ass bit by bit, every centimeter of him opening new sensations. Beckett keeps rubbing my clit, sliding his fingers down to caress my empty pussy as I writhe and moan.

I'm a mess. I'm half begging this man to fuck me harder, make me come, and I'm half whimpering, moaning, barely able to form words.

Finally, he's all the way in, cock buried up to the hilt. The edges of my vision are white with pleasure, and Beckett slides his hand to my pussy, his fingers teasing at my lips.

"Please," I whimper, the only word I can form right now.

He rubs my entrance one more time, then pushes two fingers in. I can feel the force he has to use to get even *that* inside me, my back hole stuffed completely full, but the sensation makes me grab the front of his shirt so hard I nearly rip it.

Then they both fuck me. Beckett crooks his fingers and strokes my inner wall as Kieran fucks my ass, and it's totally different than anything else I've ever done.

I'm coming in seconds. I'm coming so hard I think I might have broken reality, and as I listen to someone *scream* their names for half a second I wonder if I'm still in my coma, if this is some sort of dream.

I break. I shatter. I sob with my release, not sure if I'm even human any more, but then they stop. I don't even speak, just breathe, but Beckett gets off the bed, shedding his clothes quickly, his massive cock pointing skyward and dripping.

With one quick motion, Kieran rolls onto his back, still deep inside me. I squeal, but then I'm sitting astride him, kneeling over him, his cock shifting inside me until I moan, my own hands finding my clit and nipples.

I watch Beckett, my hips bucking as I start to ride Kieran with my ass. I can't help it, can't help touching myself, even as Beckett comes back, kneels in front of me, kissing me viciously.

He doesn't say anything, but I grab his cock, near-delirious with pleasure, and he rubs my clit and pussy again, my juices running down over Kieran's cock, still in my ass.

"Lean back," Beckett whispers, and I obey, Kieran's arms taking me in.

Beckett's breathing hitches in his chest as he slides his cock along my belly, to my mound, past my clit, against my entrance.

There's absolutely no room, Kieran's massive cock stretching me out, and I think to myself *there's no possible way Beckett can fuck me too.*

But then he thrusts, lightly, practically wedging himself inside and I feel the head of his cock pop into my entrance. Kieran and I both groan, Beckett grabbing my shoulder, breath coming in quick pants.

"Fuck, Princess, I might just come inside you right now," he moans. "God, it feels fucking perfect when you're already stuffed full."

He enters me slowly, pushing his thick length into me, grinding up against every nerve and pleasure center in my pussy until at last, somehow, they're both completely hilted inside me.

Kieran's got one arm around me, leaning against the headboard as I sit on his cock, caressing both nipples, nibbling at my ear.

"You've finally got us both," he whispers. "You like it, Princess?"

"I love it," I breathe.

"I love you," Kieran says, his lips brushing my ear. "And I love that you're our dirty princess."

His hand drifts down to my clit, and he starts rubbing me, slowly.

"I love you, too," Beckett says, and he starts to move. "And I love how much you like being shared."

I can't answer, because they both start moving together, fucking me in sync, and I can't possibly form words. All I can do is moan, whimper, pant for breath.

And come. I can barely do anything but come, almost instantly as they both start moving, but I don't stop. I come in wave after wave, shower after shower. I explode into sparks, dissolve into water, and just when I'm nearly certain I'm not even human any more, I come again.

They fuck me slow, hard, deep, *exactly* the way I need it. I can hear myself babbling but I have no idea what I'm saying, I just know that I'm coming endlessly.

Finally, Beckett whispers into my ear.

"I'm gonna come inside you," he growls, and then

instantly, he does.

A moment later Kieran explodes as well, both of them filling me at once, my body rocked between the power of their climaxes.

I'm spread wide open to them, completely and utterly vulnerable, *theirs* in a way I can't even begin to explain.

But right now, in this moment, I'm more certain than ever that there will never be anyone else for me. There can't be.

And I know they feel exactly the same way.

I collapse backward onto Kieran, and he wraps his arms around me. Beckett nuzzles his head against my shoulder, the sweat slowly trickling down my neck.

"God, I do love you," he whispers.

I just stroke his head, perfectly content, warm, cozy, and *safe* between Kieran and Beckett. I can't imagine anywhere else I'd rather be, and I know that no matter what, I'm *theirs*.

Whatever my parents say. Whatever my father says, it doesn't matter. If we have to, we'll elope.

After a long time, they both slide out and we're back on the bed. I'm on my side, facing Kieran this time, snuggled between them. He kisses me softly, tenderly, and Beckett strokes my hair.

"Kieran, Beckett," I say, finally managing to find words.

"Hmm?" Kieran murmurs.

"I love you too," I say.

They kiss me, warm and gentle, one after the other, and then we all fall asleep.

EPILOGUE

Bianca

Two Months Later

I pace across the room, inexplicably nervous even though everything is perfect. The flowers are perfect, my dress is perfect, the cake is perfect.

Even the weather decided to cooperate for once, the sunlight streaming through my dressing room's tall window.

"Stop it," Aurora says.

She's sitting along one wall, on a white couch, nursing her two-month-old daughter.

"You got your father to agree to this, and that was the hardest part," she points out. "Everything now will be smooth sailing."

I sigh, because I know she's right. Even getting my dad to let me marry *two* men at once wasn't nearly as difficult as I was afraid it would be — after my near-death scare, I think he'd have said yes to nearly anything I asked.

"But everyone's going to disapprove," I say, stomach roiling. I'm nauseous *again*, but I ignore the sensation.

Aurora's looking down, stroking the baby's cheek as she nurses.

"They're all going to be whispering, you know, *whose child is it*, what do they do at night, how can they possibly *both* be her husband..."

"And?" Aurora asks.

"And... I don't want people to talk about me?"

Aurora smiles, shifting in her seat. Her daughter's hand splays against her chest, and she takes it in her own.

"You know they're already talking, right? And they're saying all those things, and it's every bit as gross and salacious as you're afraid it is," she says.

I flush bright red. I can't *imagine* the lords and ladies of the kingdom talking about what Kieran, Beckett, and I do in bed.

"And worse, from what you've told me, they're right," she teases. "You saucy little minx, you."

"I—"

She waves one hand in the air, laughing.

"You know *I'm* all for it," she says. "Get it, girl. But they're already talking, so you may as well marry the loves of your life, sweetheart."

Her daughter detaches from her breast, waves her arms, starts looking around.

"Done?" Aurora asks softly, reattaching her nursing bra and pulling her dress back up.

I sigh.

"I know you're right," I say, my hand unconsciously going to my own belly. "I'm just nervous is all."

"Everyone gets nervous," Aurora assures me. "I was nervous, Ella says she was nervous. It's a huge day. Don't let it get to you."

There's a knock on the door, and I quickly double-check that Aurora's decent before shouting, "Come in!"

It opens. Kieran and Beckett walk in. I frown.

"You're not supposed to be here!" I say, crossing my arms. "I thought we *agreed* that you weren't going to see me before the ceremony today—"

Quietly, Aurora stands, her daughter in her arms.

"We couldn't help ourselves," Beckett grins.

"It's bad luck," I insist.

"I bet we can make it up to you," Kieran says, raising one eyebrow.

"I've gotta go, um, do some stuff that's not in this

room," Aurora says, and breezes out the door, shutting it firmly behind herself.

"Don't mess up my dress," I say, acquiescing. "Or my hair, that took someone *hours*."

Kieran grins, his face wolfish, as Beckett moves around behind me.

"We would *never*," he whispers. "We just wanted to come remind you that we've got a surprise in store for you tonight."

I bite my lip, whole body flushing. I've got no idea what it is, but they've been teasing me for a week, and every time I get wet as a waterfall.

"If you get bored during the hour-long ceremony, just imagine the possibilities," Beckett says into my ear. "We want you to think about it *all day*, Princess."

"That's all," Kieran smiles.

"You just wanted to come torture me?" I tease.

"We just wanted to come say hello," Kieran says.

Beckett puts his hand on my lower belly, protectively.

"To both of you," he says.

I swallow, putting my own hand over his.

Tell them, I think.

But you're not even sure.

Yes, you are. Tell them anyway.

"The three of us, actually," I whisper.

Kieran frowns for a moment, but then his face

lights up.

"You mean..."

"It's twins," I say. "A boy and a girl."

Beckett squeezes my belly just a little harder, wrapping his other arm around me.

"How do you know?"

I shake my head.

"I just do," I say.

He kisses the side of my neck.

"I love you," he murmurs, then pats my belly. "And I love you two."

Kieran kisses my forehead silently, but I know he means the same thing.

"We love you back," I say.

We stay like that for a long time, standing in the sunlight.

Our own little family.

ABOUT PARKER

I write obsessed, dominant, alpha heroes who stop at *nothing* to get their women - and get them dirty!

I can be found driving around my small, southern town in either my minivan or hubby's pickup truck. No one here is the wiser about my secret writing life… and I definitely prefer it that way!